MW00893929

Escape from Heart

Escape from Heart

Lynette Stark

Harcourt, Inc.
San Diego New York London

www.harcourt.com

Library of Congress Cataloging-in-Publication Data
Stark, Lynette, 1952–
Escape from Heart/by Lynette Stark.
p. cm.
Summary: Fourteen-year-old Sarah Ruth Heart describes how her self-absorbed, hypocritical uncle nearly destroys the Mennonite community over which he has become leader.
[1. Mennonites—Fiction. 2. Family life—Mississippi—Fiction. 3. Mississippi—Fiction.] I. Title.
PZ7.S79445Es 2000
[Fic]—dc 21 99-50976
ISBN 0-15-202385-2

Text set in Galliard

Designed by Lori McThomas Buley

First edition
A C E G H F D B

Printed in the United States of America

For my mom, Eileen Stark,
and with much gratitude to my agent,
Laura Rennert, of Andrea Brown Agency,
and my editor, Karen Grove

Escape from Heart

1

I WILL ALWAYS remember the year my entire world came to a sudden end, and I had to find refuge in a new one. Aunt Lila went first. Until Aunt Lila no one had ever left Heart Colony, not in over one hundred years. Mennonites are usually very happy and hardworking, but in Heart Colony we had become just hardworking. I blame my uncle, Hezekiel Whittenstone, for that, and Hezekiel is purely why we left, though I shall tell you about that in a moment, along with my serious affection for spelling words out, such as Mennonite—M-e-n-n-o-n-i-t-e. That's what we are. That is my religion and my way of life.

My name is Sarah Ruth Heart, and Heart Colony was named after my father's people. There are fifteen families and fifteen houses in Heart, not counting Widow Jacobs's. We are safely hidden away from the outside world in the northeastern corner of Mississippi, next to the Alabama line, just below the city of Tupelo. Temptation beckoned from the nearby town of SlapEasy, with its motorcycles, microwaves, and color TVs, but we are God-fearing people. Everything we need, and only what we truly need, is produced right here in the colony—food, faith, and family. I was happy with my hair pinned against my head and my dress covering all but my hands and feet. The sins of the modern world held no appeal and were especially harmful to fourteen-year-old girls like me. Or so I'd been told back then, so often that leaving the colony never crossed my mind.

I don't think it ever crossed Aunt Lila's mind until that late-summer day of the foot washing. Her husband, Hezekiel, knelt beside the dusty church road, his face reddened from spiritual exertion and the sun. A small white towel hung over his thick shoulder. A leader humbling himself before God and man, he nonetheless wore his Sunday best. The gray pants were too big and the gray shirt too small, so that in kneeling, he appeared to be crumpling. His red full-length beard, along with the shaggy rest of him, was sinking slowly into the dirt. He clutched the Bible and cast anxious looks up into the very warm sky.

In second-best clothes of brown, the deacons stood solemnly in their second-rank position for the ceremony. Their perfumed feet glistened and left damp signatures pressed into the young grass. The women stood around the men, our long, full skirts the color of bluebells in the meadow.

Everyone was waiting. All of the congregation was staring at my aunt Lila, and she knew it. She had arrived late and offered no explanation. She picked up the white basin of dirty water, tucked the jar of homemade ointment under her arm, and quietly tried to escape.

"Come back here," Hezekiel commanded his wife. "We are through with the ceremony, and yet my sons fail to appear. Where are they?"

"I told you earlier, they are in the fields." Aunt Lila's voice was steady but her hands were not. The dirty water sloshed over the sides of the basin and stained her skirt. "I forgot about the service. I sent them to pull choke weeds from the melon patch."

Several women of the church cast disapproving frowns at Lila. I looked around for my friend Joshua. He was not in the crowd. I adjusted the pins in my thin blond hair to make it appear fuller, in case he did show up. Not that it mattered to me.

"How could you forget about the foot-washing ceremony?"

Aunt Lila clutched the basin closer. "Because I've been a Mennonite in this colony all my life and I never heard of a foot-washing ceremony until you took over as leader."

The deacons were now staring intently at Hezekiel. He got up off his knees and slapped the towel at the ground.

"Although everyone is required to attend our special services, I know God forgives and understands when hard work is the cause of absence. I am proud of my sons for their hard work."

Hezekiel walked past his wife and refused to look at her. With another frustrated snap of the towel, he brushed off the streaks of dust on his pants knees. Under the thick mat of auburn hair, his ears burned red with embarrassment. Everyone was whispering, and it was once again about Aunt Lila's lack of religious fervor.

"I've never heard my sister talk to him that way before," my mother whispered to me. "I wonder why she did that."

It could have ended there, with the usual clucking of tongues and forgotten past episodes, but the ceremony had inspired Eric, the newest convert to our colony, to step forward and make an unusual request for a weekday. His dark hair was still growing out, but had not yet reached below the tips of his ears. Even in Mennonite clothes, he looked like an outsider, but perhaps it would always be that way because of his high cheekbones and the olive tint in his skin.

"I want to be baptized right now. I can't wait for Sunday."

Although no one born here ever left Heart Colony, sometimes others came in. Some were unhappy with the evils of the outside world, some *were* the evils of the outside world. Both thought of this place as an escape. I didn't know which of the two Eric was. It wasn't our way to ask or to pry. We took in anyone needing shelter, and we prodded a few to newer shelters soon enough.

I was surprised by Eric's request. It appeared to me not to be very genuine, and I had seen Eric's "new" parents whispering in his ear, prodding him to proclaim this sudden, heartfelt "inspiration."

But Hezekiel was ecstatic. His sermon about the dedication and martyrdom of the Anabaptists had been successful. His speech about sincerity and the need to be rebaptized when joining this one true church, no matter the baptisms before, had found its mark in this stranger. The disappointment caused by his sons' absence readily left his face. Those who had been persecuted centuries ago for embracing simple, unadorned Old Testament beliefs were now guiding Hezekiel's path in spirit. John the Baptist, the prophets, and the apostles from the New Testament as well—Hezekiel could feel their blessing upon him, granting him permission to call out in the name of the Father, the Son, and the Holy Spirit. The whole smiling congregation of Heart Colony went arm in arm to the creek as Aunt Lila followed, trying to talk Hezekiel out of performing the ceremony.

"I am sure the boy has been baptized before," she said.

"We do not recognize infant baptisms. How can an infant choose? Or what if it were of another church? Outside churches are not always of God, no matter the name given as proof."

"We are pourers, not immersionists. The ladle is at the church. You must use the ladle."

"This is a wonderful day. God is smiling upon my witnessing, for I have brought another to Him, ready to dedicate his life."

"My father never baptized in the creek. Many of the

congregation don't like the changes you've been making." Aunt Lila's face was white, her small head twisting this way and that as she began pleading with the others to wait until Sunday, wait until everyone was in church . . .

"Your father died over ten years ago. He is no longer the leader!" Hezekiel waved the Bible at her face. "I have been colony leader for ten good years now, and I am the third person to ever *be* chosen leader of Heart Colony, after Deacon Heart and your father, Deacon Franks. I am tired of your criticizing my leadership! We are going to the creek, and there will be much rejoicing!"

But the splashing and rejoicing came not from a free-spirited afternoon baptism but from my sly boy cousins, who had escaped a day's toil and the foot-washing ceremony by swimming naked in the creek. And who could blame them? Although this was the middle of August, these days were usually the hottest days of all the year in Mississippi. "Dog days," we called them. The temperature seldom dropped below one hundred degrees. I know. I was tired of standing around and sweating.

"Git home. Git on home." Hezekiel stood on the sagging timber bridge, yelling down at his sons. He threw his Bible.

Everyone scattered, horrified at the anger and the scandal. Even worse, my youngest cousin kept saying, "Mother said we could."

The Randolph family, which had taken Eric in as the

son promised them by God, shook their fingers at Lila and her boys. Eric fetched the wet Bible off the creek bank and tenderly wiped it off before returning it to Hezekiel.

I WAS IN THE COOL, dark hallway of Aunt Lila's house later that strange summerlike day. The scrubbed floor gleamed below my bare feet. I remember I had a pecan pie in my hand, and Mother was carrying two more just like it. Aunt Lila's voice came through the blackened wires of the back screen door. I don't remember what she said. I only remember the pleading sound of her voice and the warm smell of caramelized pecans. I heard my uncle's voice echoing from the backyard.

"The boys were idle, the way the Devil wants them to be." Hezekiel's words held an eerie quiver. "Your hand led them astray. Your hand will now guide them to righteousness."

"Go home," Mother said in a whisper to me, letting go of the screen door handle. One of the pies tilted dangerously on her arm. She tried to balance them again.

I could see Aunt Lila's backyard, now that Mother had stepped aside. All eight of my boy cousins stood in a row, at eight different levels of height. Brown hair cut in the same simple bowl style, pale blue shirts, and denim overalls. Even I couldn't tell who was who from this short distance.

"You told them they could disobey my orders. You and they have embarrassed me in front of my church, in front of God. You go on and hit them. This is what you caused." Hezekiel loomed over her. "Consider that this is nothing compared to the wrath of God on all sinners. I am saving you from that day of retribution."

Aunt Lila held a wooden board in her hands. Then she touched the small bun on top of her head, and the gesture reminded me of my mother. From a distance Aunt Lila resembled my mother and the rest of the women of Heart Colony, except that Aunt Lila's head had bald spots, the honey-colored hair was pulled so tightly. That and premature streaks of gray added a haunted look to Aunt Lila's thin face. The board slipped through her sweating hands, leaving an imprint of fingers that dried slowly on the hard wood. She bit her bottom lip and picked up the board again.

I heard sharp cracks of wood against thin flesh. The shirt of the oldest boy puffed out each time the board approached him. Holding back the tears, he kept his head bowed with shame. It wasn't until the welts on his back began to rise up to greet the wood that he finally cried. It broke out of him like a dying bird—a strangled, high-pitched chirp.

Lila wiped her hands on her heavy cotton skirt. Drops of perspiration outlined the sharp edge of her skull. She gripped the board again. The boys visibly tensed. She began again. The corners of her mouth drooped low and full, catching the angry tears as she moved to each younger child.

The youngest boy burst out crying before the board even touched him. Because he was only five, Aunt Lila moved the board slower. Tears were now streaming down her face. She turned pleadingly to her husband.

"You did not hit them hard enough," he said sternly, taking the board from her. "And why don't you tell me why you were late to the ceremony today?" The thick red hair of his beard rested against the circles of sweat on his brown work shirt. He raised his arm and the tightened muscles from years of hard toil in the fields began to work.

Whack, whack. The board fell upon Aunt Lila's shoulders, her back, her arms. Mother's fingertips grasped at my dress sleeve, and a small sound of alarm breathed out of her. We stood there watching guiltily in the hallway, unable to do anything.

My uncle was smiling as he hit Aunt Lila. I remember that. I wondered foolishly if we could run out and save her, but Mother's clutch forbade it. I wanted to comfort Aunt Lila, and yet, the only thing I did when she ran sobbing into the house was hand her a pecan pie.

The screen door slammed. Uncle Hezekiel began beating the boys again, starting with my littlest cousin and going up the row one by one. We could hear it but no longer looked.

Aunt Lila stared down at the pecan pie and said matter-of-factly, "I'm leaving. I can't take my children with me. If I do, he'll follow, and he will kill them and me. He only beats them because of things he says I cause them to do."

Mother handed her the other two pies. Aunt Lila

could barely hold them. The red welts on her arms were swelling into puffy purple lines. You could see the edge of pain in her eyes.

"Hannah, this time I'm really going. I have to. Help me. Promise me you will look after my boys."

"Give Hezekiel and the boys some pie. We're going home now." Mother firmly grabbed me by the shoulder and led me away from Aunt Lila. The heavy swish of our skirts echoed down the empty hallway. Behind us the kitchen door creaked open slowly. Glancing over my shoulder, I saw Aunt Lila give my cousin Mary Helen the pies.

Mother held open the front screen door and admonished me not to turn around and stare.

But when I sneaked a look back, Aunt Lila was all alone in the hallway. She was staring at the polished wood planks of her house floor as if they were something holy, descended from Heaven.

"Why can't we help her?" I did not understand my mother's coldness.

"Her children need her, and the world outside is a bad place to be. Don't talk of this again—to anyone."

Mother's forehead was full of deep worry lines. *How could the outside world be worse for Aunt Lila than what she has every day in her own house?* I wondered. I hurried across the yard behind my mother. She no longer seemed to notice me.

The white, two-storied houses of Heart Colony rested peacefully among the hills and along the narrow paved road. The sunset painted warm shadows across the high, straight walls of the houses on the next hill. No one was outdoors except for Mother and me. Everyone was escaping the heat by settling in the cooler back rooms for supper, and then early sleep. I thought about my cousins and wondered if they would be allowed to eat that evening.

It smelled like rain, coming in from the direction of the cornfields. Standing on this highest colony peak near my house in early evening usually brought me close to God's breath. He was pleased, reassured. In the midst of a corrupt, indifferent world, our colony had remained in His total service. But this night I could not feel that.

All I could feel was the warm tar of the asphalt squishing between my toes as I crossed the road to our house. Mother leaned against the cedar tree in our front yard and inspected her feet. I hurried to the porch steps and was past the narrow posts of the porch and almost to the front door when she called out, "Sarah Ruth, you will not go into the house with tar on your feet."

Reluctantly, I returned to the yard. I wiped my feet in the soft grass and then followed my mother into the house. Although Mother was obviously not going to discuss Aunt Lila's plea for help, I knew it was on her mind as she worked silently in the kitchen. I helped her cook supper, and it was a good thing I did. With a loud hiss, the water for the butter beans boiled over and hit the flames of the gas burner. Mother stared, unhearing, as I moved the pan to a cooler burner.

At the supper table my family ate silently. Usually Mother kept the conversation lively. Tonight she hardly talked or ate any food. Buttered crumbs of corn bread fell from my father's open mouth and clung to his long brown beard. My brother Adam slurped his iced tea noisily. Father glared at him, then cleared his throat and wiped away the crumbs with his sleeve.

"Hezekiel says Sarah Ruth must quit school."

I gasped loudly and looked pleadingly at my mother. The others put down their forks and stared at me. My little sister, Rachel, was not smirking like the boys were.

"School just started," I protested. "I've only been for three weeks."

"I've put off saying it for as long as I could. Can't put it off no more."

"She can't quit right now." Mother lowered her head respectfully.

"You and I quit when we were her age. We were needed to work the fields."

Mother lifted her head and stared straight into Father's eyes. "I remember you cried, because you loved school. You were smart. I remember."

His face flushed from the praise, but he kept his voice stern. "This isn't about smart, or you and me. Hezekiel has deemed this be done."

"Why? This is a Mennonite school. She is almost finished. She's *in* eighth grade. It doesn't hinder her chores at home."

"It hinders us in the colony."

"Your good friend James Ackerman supports the school," Mother said.

"James Ackerman has no children in the school."

"Many people in the colony look up to his wisdom. They say he is second in command, next to Hezekiel. Just because he has no children doesn't mean James Ackerman doesn't know what's good for the children of our colony. What do you have against this school?"

"The government has taken over our school, teaching obedience to a nation instead of obedience to God, forcing our children under the compulsory law to attend a school we no longer completely control."

"Then Hezekiel shouldn't have accepted the government offer of money and books to run the school," Mother said. "It's his own fault if he is unhappy. It's your fault if you're unhappy. You are a deacon. You voted to accept the offer."

"But I *didn't* vote for that teacher," Father said stubbornly.

"Mrs. Monroe was teaching our children how to read and write, things the children should learn. Before everyone took their children out of school at Hezekiel's command, Sarah Ruth won the classroom spelling bee. I think that's why some of the parents want us to pull her out—because she's smarter than their children. Their children couldn't do the work. But Sarah Ruth could."

"That teacher is not a Mennonite, and she's a bad influence. Tell me you don't see a change in Sarah Ruth. That woman has filled Sarah Ruth's head with false temptations of other places and things that don't matter nohow to any of us."

Father began to eat again. The fork scraped against his teeth.

"Then our daughter is bad? That's what Hezekiel said to you?" Mother jerked the bread basket off the table as Father reached for it.

"Sarah Ruth must quit school, and so must Adam and Eli."

My two younger brothers looked at each other and grinned. I kicked Eli under the table before tearfully making my exit from the room. It was then that I first hated Heart Colony. I didn't want to be a Mennonite, or at least not a Heart Mennonite.

My little sister, Rachel, stood quietly inside the bedroom door as I cried.

"I won the spelling bee. I was the best one at the school. I *hate* Hezekiel!" I yelled.

It made me feel better to glare out the window at his house. The rage inside burned from my eyes.

"I'm only six. I didn't get to go to the Mennonite school," Rachel said softly, and left the room.

If it wasn't for the intense anger I was throwing at the next rooftop, I would have comforted Rachel and told her that one day she would be old enough to go to school and hopefully by then Hezekiel would be gone. But I didn't. I was secretly knee-deep in sin, wishing and heaping a multitude of curses upon Hezekiel. I began spelling out my curses, feeling the power of my anger and my spelling-bee winner knowledge.

"Vengeance . . . v-e-n-g-e-a-n-c-e . . . vile . . . v-i-l-e . . . animosity . . . a-n-i-m-o-s-i-t-y . . . boils and warts . . . b-o-i—"

In the distance, away from Heart Colony, a lone figure in blue walked suddenly from the okra fields and headed to the main road. My heart beat fast. *Aunt Lila!* Was she really going to do it? I turned to go tell Mother but stopped.

I went back to the window and watched the escape. My aunt's thin body was stooped over, the sorrowed hands pressed against her face, as if she was crying bitterly. The long blue dress caught with the wind, revealing the heavy brown sandals that our ladies wore when selling vegetables at the farmers market in SlapEasy. As twilight descended Aunt Lila disappeared over the next hill, swallowed up by the modern world. I shivered out of fear and envy.

2

IT MUST HAVE been a pretty day outside, but who would notice when it was the last day of school ever? I felt very sad and lost in that small brick building. I was going to miss the round glass window, the metal desks that were so cold in the winter. I would miss the feel of chalk dust on my hand, and the smell of disinfectant forever being mopped over the tile floors. The schoolroom was filled with colors. Pink, yellow, and green roll-out maps on the walls always glowed brightly upon us as we sat there in brown clothing and pinned-up hair.

I picked up a short piece of yellow chalk. One last time I had to write my name on the chalkboard. I remembered the day Mrs. Monroe had brought a whole box of colored chalk so we could draw the layers of the earth. I had laid the red chalk sideways to draw the curved ridges of the crust evenly. Mrs. Monroe said I was like an artist. I looked at my work now. The loops in my *A*s were shaky and slanted, but I hoped my teacher would never erase this.

Mrs. Monroe studied my face, trying to understand. "But what about the county spelling bee? The county officials finally ruled you were eligible. I know you could win. It's the third Saturday of September. That's only a few weeks from now."

I stared at her short dark curls. My brother Eli used to tell everyone that Mrs. Monroe was a man-woman, because of her short hair. *I* knew, however, that in the outside world, Mrs. Monroe was considered beautiful.

"I was glad enough to win the spelling bee *here*. Wouldn't mean anything to win anywhere else." I tried, but I couldn't put any conviction into my words.

"Wouldn't *mean* anything?"

"No." A lump rose in my throat. I remember how hard I had cried when my first-place blue ribbon was thrown away. I had lied to Mrs. Monroe and said my parents pinned it over the front door.

"Where are all the others? Why isn't anyone showing up anymore? Are they coming back?" There was a tough sparkle to Mrs. Monroe's eyes. I knew she already had the answers.

"Thank you for teaching me." I reached for the stack of notebooks with my name on them.

"I did everything they asked. I took the flag off my desk. I haven't discussed politics in here. I don't see what they object to."

"*I* don't think you're a bad person."

Mrs. Monroe gave me a rueful smile, then began inspecting the lead pencils, noisily pulling them out of the tin can on her desk and pointedly dropping them back in. Little *ping-ping*s filled the room.

She had taken the American flag off her desk, but she hadn't got rid of it as Hezekiel had requested. It was in her desk drawer, on top of the gold-framed picture of a man in uniform. I'd found it one day when searching for chalk.

"You know quite well what your future will be, don't you?" she said.

I scarcely breathed. This anger I didn't expect. I wanted her to cry a little, so I could always remember it.

"I was never trying to change your life, or this community. There are many things I admire about the Heart Colony way of doing things, but this... this . . ."

"We have no need—"

"You are *told* you have no need of school, but think, how will Heart Colony survive in the future? You depend on the outside world for certain things, and you must keep pace, or you'll be wiped out." *Ping,* another pencil went into the can.

"But we're not a part of the outside world."

"You *are* a part, whether you like it or not. That is my point, Sarah Ruth. And it's not that nice of a world out there sometimes, but sometimes it's not so nice around here. There's good in both. There's bad in both. You need an education to be able to tell the difference."

"We *know* the difference."

"Not too long ago the colony bought a new tractor. Remember that? Paid cash for it, signed the paper, but Hezekiel couldn't read the document. He didn't even ask for a receipt. Where is that new tractor? It was never delivered, was it? Hezekiel couldn't prove he paid the salesman, and the document he signed was really not a bill of sale. The salesman he paid disappeared with the money, so the colony is stuck with that same old tractor with the heavy cart permanently attached. Wouldn't a little education have helped in that situation? How many hours in the field did your family work, to throw that money away because Hezekiel couldn't read the fine print or tell the difference between a postdated lease and an actual bill of sale?"

"The outside world—"

"The outside world has a few crooks. So why don't you learn how to protect yourselves? Education protects. That's why Mr. Ackerman supports the school. He's the one who has to drive that old tractor all the time. If it wasn't for the kindness of James Ackerman, this school wouldn't be here. And now that there is no new tractor, he's working even harder to see that all the Mennonite children can read—and understand everything they read. Do you know he even gives me extra baskets of vegetables with my pay so that I'll stay? He wants a school. He asks me about the progress of the students all the time. He keeps up with it. He is very proud of you especially."

"He's proud of me?" I was more than surprised.

"Yes, because you're not afraid to learn. That's what he said. He's afraid the colony might die out without more children like you."

Mrs. Monroe let go of the pencil can and walked to the big filing cabinet. She pulled out the top drawer. The back of her navy blue dress had rows and rows of tiny pleats: a wasteful sin. I really liked it.

"Sarah Ruth," she said, turning around. "I know this isn't really how you feel or what you want. I know what a smart young woman you are. I know you want to stay in school. I wish I could help you. I wish you would ask. Here."

She motioned for me to take a small black plastic box.

"All you've ever been told has been the bad things of the outside world. I want you to know some of the good things, so you can have them at Heart Colony, so Heart Colony will continue to grow and thrive and be a place of joy. I wish some of Heart Colony would rub off on the rest of the world, such as your aversion to war. Think how nice it would be to share all the good of both worlds." Mrs. Monroe smiled warmly at me. "You're the best student I've ever taught, at any school. Please, take this tape recorder as a gift for the hours of pleasure you have given me by learning so eagerly. Perhaps you can use it at home for playing learning tapes or listening to music. There's a tape in here of the opera *Carmen,* by Bizet. It's quite beautiful."

I hesitated, but Mrs. Monroe was walking toward me, holding out the tape recorder. There were the hoped-for tears finally in her eyes.

MOTHER WAS SITTING on the front porch, shelling butter beans, when I returned. Across the road the colony's station wagon was gone from Aunt Lila's driveway. I wiped off the tears that had fallen during my journey home.

"Where's the car?" I asked.

"Hezekiel has gone to town today." Mother was very nervous.

"Aunt Lila ran away."

"No, I'm sure she got up early this morning and walked to town for supplies and didn't tell anyone."

"No." I sat down on the corner of the porch and swung my legs back and forth over the edge. I hugged the notebooks and tape recorder to me. "She ran away last night. I saw her."

"You must never tell anyone that you saw her." Mother's shoulders drooped. She sighed deeply. A brown pod fell from her fingers into the paper bag at her feet.

"Wouldn't Hezekiel and her children notice that she wasn't in the house last night?" I asked.

"Perhaps they thought she was hiding in the back field. She's done that before. You've done that before."

"But not because of a beating. I was only playing a joke on Eli."

"None of us found it too funny." Mother snapped the last butter bean pod and let it fall into the paper bag. She quickly flapped the contents of her apron into another bag and smiled with satisfaction at the freshly snapped beans.

"Where will Aunt Lila go?"

"She has somewhere safe, that's all that can be said." Mother picked up a handful of field peas and began shelling again. "What's that thing in your hands?"

"Mrs. Monroe gave it to me. It's a tape recorder. It plays music."

"Music?" Mother looked quickly across the yard and then down the road at the other colony houses. "We can't have music anymore. Not since Hezekiel."

I pushed the first button. The tape recorder clicked once and then stopped. I tried to remember what Mrs. Monroe had shown me. I pushed the second button, and the sweetest sounds I had ever heard spilled across the open porch.

"It works like a record player." Mother nodded, understanding. "I like that music. It's beautiful. Reminds me of trees in the back fields when they're moving with the wind, right before a night thunderstorm."

Hush, I thought. *I want to listen.*

"They're crying. Now the trees are crying."

Hush, Mother. I shut my eyes. I let the music cry for me, too, as it opened up my soul. Deeply planted sorrow floated upward, freeing itself, a long strand of silver snaking its way throughout the sky.

"The county officials ruled I could enter the big spelling bee," I said, my eyes still shut. I could reach out and touch the softness in the air.

"You heard what your father said."

"They need to know we're smart, that we can read, so they won't cheat us, like with that tractor."

"Don't do this to me, Sarah Ruth. I can't do anything about it. One day your father will be the leader of Heart Colony, that is my hope story. Then it will be easier for all of us."

I opened my eyes. "I could go, and no one from here would ever know."

Mother shook her head. "No. Oh— Listen to that!" She playfully moved her head back and forth. "The music is dancing in my head!"

I knew what she was doing, but I pretended to have forgotten the spelling bee question, too. "My teacher said the word *orchestra* originally meant 'to dance.' "

"I wonder if it is sinful to dance in your head, where no one can see it?" Mother was serious once again. "Don't tell anyone my hope story. Not now, anyway."

I promised I wouldn't and wondered how long she would be hoping. I punched the first button and the music stopped. The music had freed me, filled me with new ideas.

"Although I'm not going to the county spelling bee, can I still practice my words?"

Mother, not paying the slightest attention, said yes.

My brothers and sister were coming in from the fields. Barefoot and sunburned, dragging caps and a bonnet, they toted big wooden baskets with crooked wire handles. The baskets were full.

"Hide that music thing before your brothers see it,"

Mother said. "You probably need to return it to that teacher so we won't be in any more trouble with Hezekiel."

I slipped an empty paper sack over the tape recorder and hid it in the barrel of field peas by Mother's chair, knowing it wouldn't stay there long, and knowing I would never take it back to the teacher.

"We picked lots of beans!" Adam said, the dirt clinging to his straight blond hair. "We had lots of fun. We didn't miss school a bit!"

He and Eli climbed up on the porch and headed straight for the barrel with my tape recorder in it.

"No. These are field peas." I kept my hands firmly over the top.

They shrugged and moved over to the next barrel. They emptied their baskets into the barrel and put the top on. Then they stood on either side and began rolling the barrel carefully off the porch.

"Can we work the beans again tomorrow?" Adam asked. "Me and Eli marked our rows. I pulled the most weeds. I won."

Mother smiled. "Work is good for you, but you mustn't make games of it. Our lives depend on this food."

"You used to teach us games to play while working in the fields," Eli said crossly.

"Hezekiel goes to all the fields every day now," Mother reminded them. "He doesn't want any foolishness."

"What about that one?" Adam pointed to the barrel with my tape recorder.

"I'll move it," I said a little too eagerly, and soon began to regret my decision.

Mother and Rachel followed the boys as they rolled the barrel to the food cellar. I struggled far behind, half walking and half rolling the barrel. I finally reached the cellar, which was built into the ground next to the house; its dirt floor was cool, soothing. After a hot day in the sun, standing in the food cellar was as close to sinless pleasure as you could get.

The boys set their barrel next to the sweet potato bins. The job completed, they hurried out. I carefully placed my barrel next to the beans and then checked inside the sack to ensure my tape recorder was intact. Little Rachel stood there quietly, breathing deeply, her face so pale that you could see the blue veins underneath. Mother watched her carefully. Rachel was always fighting a bad case of allergies.

"Rachel, you needing to stay?"

Rachel shook her head no at Mother and followed us out of the cellar.

As we walked around to the front, I saw the colony's station wagon was back in Aunt Lila's driveway. It had been such a beautiful car, a metallic, gold-flecked color. But now it was painted a flat, unshiny light brown—everything, including the chrome rims and bumper. The car looked like a mud dauber's nest on wheels. "Hezekiel's Wheels" we sometimes called it, but Mother said that was sacrilegious.

Mother froze at the sight of the brown dauber. I knew what she was thinking: Hezekiel had fetched Aunt Lila home.

But I didn't think so. If he had forced her to come home, he would be busy with her. He wouldn't have had enough time to neatly chain both sides of the car doors together and hook up the long chain around the tree to the car. Hezekiel wasn't afraid of some outsider stealing the only colony car. He was just afraid of some of us using it. But my mother had a key to the chains, thanks to Aunt Lila.

"Wait here." Mother went across the road, the worry lines scrawling deeply across her wide forehead.

I watched her pound on Aunt Lila's front screen door. Over and over again she knocked. A fearful thought began to fill me. Then I dismissed it. Hezekiel needed his wife and children to work the fields and keep the house. He wasn't stupid.

It took forever for him to answer the door and talk to Mother. His gray shirt and pants were stained with sweat, but that was his fault for taking the air conditioner out of the car, deeming it another one of those "sinful luxuries."

"The boys were just being boys," I heard her say.

Hezekiel seemed to lower his voice for no one but Mother to hear. Then he went back inside again.

Mother seemed satisfied with her brief conversation with Hezekiel, and she hurried back across the road.

"He couldn't find Lila," she said with a mixture of terror and relief. "We are not to mention her name again."

"What does that mean?" I didn't know if Mother could really do that.

"She is to be shunned. You know how that works."

"He took his gun. I can see it propped against the dashboard."

"You know why he takes his gun when he travels. His father was killed in the outside world."

"What if he really found Aunt Lila, and he killed her?"

Mother turned furiously upon me. "Never say that! And never mention her! She is my sister and I love her, but she is shunned."

"But he could have killed her. He beat her really bad yesterday. Didn't you see those bruises? How can you ignore that if you love her?"

"She ran off with the driver of the delivery truck that brings supplies here. That's who she was with when everybody else was at the foot-washing ceremony. This Sunday she was going to have to confess to the Church." Mother was wiping a tear from her eye. "Now do you understand?"

"No." I truly did not.

"And why not?"

I didn't look at her as I walked into the house. I knew I was absolutely right.

"Because I saw her leave. Alone."

3

THE THOUGHT OF HEZEKIEL searching me out and killing me stifled my brave plans for the county spelling bee. Aunt Lila's children did not emerge from the house for several days. Hezekiel went around the colony all mournful-like, but I knew it secretly thrilled him that Aunt Lila was gone. There was a certain swagger to his walk, and the women of Heart Colony were baking all day long for "poor Hezekiel and his children."

By Hezekiel's orders we gathered in his kitchen and did canning for three hectic days. Every woman and young girl in the colony crowded in, even Rachel, whose job was to test the sealed lids for air bumps. The food would be sent to a starving Mennonite colony in South America. How Hezekiel had heard of it, I don't know, but he said it was our duty to help the new colony establish itself. We sterilized, cooked, poured, and sealed in that hot kitchen. Not once did anyone mention Aunt Lila, though it was her name on the bottom of all the canning jars. Aunt Lila had always been so proud of those jars, because she had a full matched set. The jars had a tiny diamond design around the bottom of the glass, and if Aunt Lila gave you a jar of pepper jelly for a special occasion, she expected that special jar to be returned when empty. Now the jars were going where they'd probably never come back. The thought of it saddened me. But then, Aunt Lila wasn't coming back, either.

I finished blanching the lima beans and poured the hot water out. While watching the temperature gauges rattle on top of the pressure cookers for the jellies, I fashioned a set of false teeth out of leftover sealing paraffin. I could amuse my brothers with this toy, I thought, putting it in my pocket.

Naomi Schumpert handed me a colander full of mustard greens and told me to wash them so they could also be prepared. I did, but I hated doing that to South America, after they had gotten their expectations up for good food.

The canning was hard work, but there was time to catch up on weeks of news. If Hezekiel only knew all the gossip and laughter stealing out from that kitchen, South America would have ended up starving.

This was how it used to be in the colony, Mother said. Everyone enjoying their work and each other's company. I couldn't say I completely enjoyed it. There were other things I'd rather have done.

It was nice, though, when Hezekiel popped in to inspect our work and rewarded us with ice-cream sandwiches he had specially brought in from SlapEasy. He had caught the Brammlett woman not working. She was sitting in a chair rocking her baby. We all held our breath, but he never yelled. He peered down at the baby and expressed concern that it might be ill instead of fussy, and then he gave us our ice-cream sandwiches and left. Perhaps I had been wrong about him, I began to think.

I HAD MANAGED without school for almost a week, and it began to hurt less. Father said Mrs. Monroe continued to come to an empty classroom and sit every day, waiting. He wondered what Hezekiel and the deacons would have to do to run her out.

There was *nothing* they could do, I could have told them that. She *liked* waiting. She was waiting for that man in the uniform to come home, too, I was sure of it, and there was no telling how long he'd been gone. The picture was old.

In the distance the broken hum of the old tractor bumped through the back fields. I had finished my chores for the day. All the clothes were washed and hanging on the line, the fat sun squeezing the water out of them. From the side window of my bedroom I could see the road and the tall green rows of okra plants next to it. I could also see a young man standing there in the okra fields. He stared up at me, enraptured. In his hands he twirled a yellow flower, like one

I had found earlier on the porch steps. His faded denim overalls were dampened with sweat; blue work shirt and no shoes, his brown hair cut in the bowl style, Joshua Mueller looked like all the other men and boys of the colony. Only he was different.

I knew he was carefully courting me, so I leaned over, pretending not to see, and shut the window. The reflection of the glass was my only chance for a mirror. I unpinned the top of my hair and let a blond ponytail dangle down. Out of the corner of my eye, I could see Joshua still watching. With my fingers I held the ponytail taut and teased my hair higher and higher until it resembled an angry squirrel's tail. I repinned the bun. My hair was the highest it had ever been. It could have been a hairy skyscraper, as tall as any building Mrs. Monroe had shown us in pictures of a city.

The door opened to my room and my cousin Mary Helen stood staring at me, appalled.

"Your hair! You've been teasing your hair!" Mary Helen's dark brown locks were twisted tightly against her scalp. She had the most beautiful hair of all, thick and curly. I was glad she kept it in a bun.

"You must comb out your bun and twist it down tightly. My father will—"

"Hezekiel does not own my hair."

"You go against God's bidding with your vanity. Fire and brimstone will greet you upon your death."

I looked at her incredulously. "For teasing my hair?"

Mary Helen nodded. Her eyes were a pale green, and there were dark shadows underneath.

"That's silly." I teased a loose strand even higher. "And it's stupid. I'm too smart. Besides, Hezekiel is the most sinful man I know."

Some of the fire returned to Mary Helen's eyes. She put her hands on her hips. I noticed a small roll of fat below the waistband, and she was only two years older than me. "My father isn't sinful. He's the supreme leader of our church."

"He beats your brothers all the time, and"—I took a deep breath—"he killed your mother."

Mary Helen gasped. I had gone too far. Now she would run and tell her father, and I would be punished severely.

"She isn't dead, and I can't talk about her," Mary Helen said, pointing her finger at me. "But when you moved your arms up like that, I saw skin! You *know* that's wrong. When you raise up, men can see your underarm!"

The long sleeves of our dresses were unbearable in warm weather. I had made small ventilation openings and usually kept my arms down when in the presence of others.

"My sleeve tore when I was picking corn."

"You must stitch it back immediately. I'll help." She began searching for a needle and thread in all my personal possessions, close to my spelling notebook.

"I'll do that." I pushed her out of the way and pretended to search. "Doesn't it bother you not to be able to talk about your mother?"

"Why is it so hot in here?" Mary Helen walked over to the shut window and opened it. "There."

She smiled suddenly and poked her head out the window. "How strange! Joshua is staring up at me." She waved.

A twinge of jealousy, a very nasty one, sent me flying to that window. All was well. Joshua wasn't looking at her. He preferred to stare at me.

I would have casually pointed that out, but I saw Hezekiel turning the corner of the row, a long gardening tool in his hand. He didn't see us, but he spotted Joshua. He shielded his eyes from the sun and frowned.

Joshua never heard him sneaking up so fast behind. Hezekiel raised the hoe. *Thwack!* He hit him squarely on the back of the head. The yellow flower fell from Joshua's hand.

Thwack, thwack. The metal blade of the hoe hooked into Joshua's back, knocking him to the ground, although it was clear he wasn't being hit full-strength. He lay there helplessly, his body convulsing with every sharp blow. Dirt mixed with the sweat on his body, turning him into a muddy mess. Blood trickled down from his forehead.

"Don't!" I screamed out.

Hezekiel looked up at the bedroom window and scowled. Instantly Joshua saw his chance. He struggled to his feet and plowed into Hezekiel, fists punching.

"Now look at what you've done!" Mary Helen was

so afraid, her teeth chattered. "Joshua deserved that. He's been saying untrue things about my father, and he's been warned once to stop. And he should have been working instead of staring up at your window. That's a sin."

Outside, Hezekiel had won the battle. But the dull thud of the hoe blade struck over and over again—sometimes to break up the soil, sometimes to break up a defiant soul.

A shiny white sports car zoomed down the winding country road, slowing as it passed Hezekiel standing over his conquest. Now he was hitting Joshua lightly with the wooden handle of the hoe. The car braked.

"The sinful world," I said to Mary Helen, though seeking the truth for myself, "does not understand our peaceful way of life." I pointed to the car. Hezekiel was also watching it suspiciously. He threw the hoe into the field and walked away. The car drove off. There was no response from Mary Helen.

I heard my bedroom door slam shut, but I didn't care. I looked down at Joshua and prayed from my window, *Please don't die. You're the only brave one at Heart Colony. I will help you.* But as I ran downstairs and opened the back door, Joshua's mother came to him with a bucket of water and some wet rags. My mother was with her and apparently had fetched her. The two women washed Joshua's face with the cold cloths, and then cleaned the bloody dirt from his hair and neck. At last Joshua stirred. His father appeared and helped him from the field.

Some of Hezekiel's insights as leader were miraculous—tearing down outhouses and installing indoor plumbing, allowing necessary electrical appliances like stoves, washers, and lights. There was a real need for those. But I saw no need for the beatings. I knew Satan was everywhere and in everything and the beatings drove him out, but it seemed to me someone needed to drive Satan out of Hezekiel.

THERE WAS AN EMPTY CHAIR that evening at the supper table. Father had gone upstairs with a wet rag to ward off another headache. Sometimes the headaches were so severe he had to lie in bed covered with heavy quilts to block out the noise and light.

Mother would tiptoe into his room and change the warm rag on his head for a cool one. Sometimes she placed a poultice on the back of his neck after massaging his face and shoulders.

"My turn." Rachel pushed a chair up to the sink so she could wash dishes.

"Do you still have those spelling words to practice?" Mother asked me.

I went upstairs for the notebooks under the bed.

Adam and Eli ran past me as I came back down the stairs. Adam was chomping at Eli with the wax teeth in his hand.

"Stop it!" Mother came into the hall and scolded them. "Your father is sick."

Then she turned to me. "Hand me the spelling words."

"Am I in trouble for keeping them?"

"No," said my mother with a mysterious smile. "I thought we'd go over them, if anything should suddenly change."

"Hezekiel might change his mind about school?"

"No." Mother pulled out a big stew pot and set it on the stove. "Remember my hope story?"

"Hezekiel is stepping down as leader?"

"No." Mother lowered her voice so that Rachel could not hear. "There are those who plan to oust Hezekiel and put your father in his place. Joshua's mother told me. Nobody should have the right to beat someone's children like that, nor to keep them from going to school. That is not the true Mennonite way."

Then it was settled. I would be going to that spelling bee. I handed the notebooks to my mother. She read the words to me as she cooked and I spelled.

"Hygienic...h-y-g-i-e-n-i-c...superstitious...s-u-p-e-r-s-t-i-t-i-o-u-s."

Sometimes she stumbled on a word and blushed, embarrassed. I'd pick up the notebook and apologize for my shortcomings in penmanship.

"Individualism, that's the word," I said. "I-n-d-i-v—"

This time the word didn't matter. She had left her dreams of Father being the new leader and was noticing the world as it was for the present. She pointed a dripping spoon at me.

"Why is your hair so tall today?" She didn't appreciate my hairy skyscraper.

"Individualism. That spelling word I just used."

"I'm not exactly sure what that means, but I'm sure that around here it doesn't mean you can wear your hair like that. Go comb it out before your father sees it."

4

DARK STORM CLOUDS draped across our colony and sent the men scrambling through the gray-gritty gauze of the morning. There was so much to be done in the back fields before the rain. Plows had to be covered with big plastic sheets. Tin livestock troughs clanked as they were dragged behind the tractor across stony pastures to higher ground. Weaker crop stalks were being reinforced and tied to wooden stakes.

I was busy, too. While everyone was preparing for the rain, Mother and I were huddled by the forbidden school. The rough bricks plucked at Mother's hair bun when she leaned against the wall. With arms hugged stubbornly in front of her, she refused to smile and refused to let me enter the building. The skies overhead darkened and rumbled.

"There's a letter about the spelling bee on top of the

work sheets. The competition will be at SlapEasy High School in the auditorium," Mrs. Monroe said, emerging from the doorway. Her hands held a big stack of papers. "Hope they don't blow away." She kept them pinned down with her chin. "I'm sorry they aren't stapled together. I can't find my stapler."

I knew where that stapler was. My cheeks warmed to a guilty pink as I climbed the bottom step and reached up. "There must be a *million* words to learn!"

Mrs. Monroe smiled. "You know most of them."

Mother's eyes were sweeping up and down my teacher. She was horrified at everything, from the pointed toes of Mrs. Monroe's lime green shoes to the magical swirls of brown, green, and white in the carefully draped scarf. Mother shook her head rather unkindly.

I wondered how Mother would look in Mrs. Monroe's clothes and a little bit of that powder and lipstick. I wondered how *I* would look.

"I could drive you to the spelling bee," Mrs. Monroe offered.

"No. I will take Sarah Ruth, should we decide to go."

"*If* you decide to go?" Mrs. Monroe stepped down and put her arm around me. Shirking off the embrace, I glanced back worriedly at my mother. Mrs. Monroe kept smiling, though. "Wouldn't it be wonderful if everyone could see how smart the children of Heart Colony are?"

"It isn't...allowed," Mother said hesitantly.

"What isn't? Going to the spelling bee, or showing how smart you are, or both? *Tell* me. Before coming to this corner of the state, I prepared myself fully. I studied your beliefs. I talked to other Mennonites, and then I get here and in many ways you're not like other Mennonites at all."

I was stunned. We weren't like other Mennonites?

"I've accepted the fact that *this* Mennonite school goes only to the eighth grade and the government allows it. I've tried to remedy that by cramming a high school education into an eighth grader's brain. Apparently you aren't aware that in other parts of the country, some Mennonites promote school along with a study of the scriptures, and there are Mennonite colleges! Imagine yourself at one of those, Sara Ruth!"

I looked up eagerly at my mother. She blinked, disbelieving.

Mrs. Monroe sighed heavily. "I've put away the flag. I've been careful about what I say, never mentioning either the church or the state. *Still* I'm not allowed to teach, and you aren't allowed to do things you're wanting to do. I think you're constantly living in fear. How can you live like this?"

"How can you dress like that?" With a slight tip of her head, Mother walked away, quite satisfied with herself.

The sudden rain prevented an apology from me, and I had no choice but to run after Mother.

Mother and I dodged raindrops and newly formed

mud puddles as we darted across the fields, trying to keep the spelling papers dry.

THE RAINS CONTINUED throughout the night, building into strong winds and stinging downpours. Part of the tin roof came off the long chicken house two fields over. It rippled noisily through the air and landed in a tree. The plastic sheets ripped off the sides of the chicken house and wrapped around the trees in the field. One sheet of plastic came as far up as our yard. It clung to the stakes of the tomato vines and threatened to enfold and smooth over all of our tender garden.

I thought it could be the ghost of Aunt Lila seeking revenge for her death, and I really wished my uncle Hezekiel's house was further down the road. The metal meat hooks on the back porch creaked in warning, back and forth. Father made all of us come downstairs. If it got much worse, he said, we would fight our way through the storm to the food cellar.

The electricity went off. Mother lit the oil lamp. The base of the glass, which held the wick, was hot. When Mother wasn't looking Eli and I played a game of who could touch the glass the longest without getting burned.

A loud rumbling caused all of us to look toward the dark front window. But instead of a tornado, car headlights passed by.

A flash of blue lightning showed us it was the brown station wagon, Hezekiel at the wheel.

"He's a fool," Mother said, whispering it only to me.

I was glad he was going, but I didn't want to admit to my mother why. Maybe I was imagining it, but within a few minutes of Hezekiel's leaving, the storm eased up.

The electricity was still off, and the heavy rain had soaked through the tiles on our roof. We could hear it dripping into small puddles in the attic. Father said tomorrow he would get some tar and flashing from the supply barn and fix the shingles.

"Tell them a story," Mother said, touching his shoulder softly, "until the storm blows out."

Father sat down on the floor and gathered us closer to him so we could hear over the rain. Rachel cuddled into his lap and Mother sat nearby, smiling approvingly at the words of wisdom in his story. Father made the Old Testament exciting, much scarier than the storm. The story of Daniel was one of his favorites to tell.

"...and because of this trickery by others, Daniel was cast into a den of roaring, hungry lions."

My brother Adam made a huge snarl, his fingers pulling apart his mouth, and growled at all of us.

"Was he afraid?" Rachel asked, shrinking back from Adam.

"No. He believed in God and would not denounce Him even in the face of death. For this loyalty God sent His angels into the cave to shut the mouths of the lions, and Daniel was spared."

"What if Daniel were in a tornado?" Adam asked carefully.

"He would know not to be afraid," Father said.

When the storm ended, we could see that the brown station wagon was back in Hezekiel's driveway. It had a crack in the windshield.

ON SUNDAY MORNING the most beautiful, pink-edged sun broke through the darkened sky. Its long white arms streamed softly to the dirt road in the center of the colony, where the solemn worshipers gathered. The sky flowed with a brightness.

As we walked we were like a fallen rain cloud. The women wore gray dresses, the men gray shirts and gray trousers, all of it made from the same humble cloth. My brother Adam kept stretching his neck upward, giraffelike. The shirt squeezed up higher and higher in response. Mother would soon have to sew Adam a new one, or give him to a family that had larger hand-me-downs.

Heart Colony Church had a fresh coat of white paint. It looked nice, though Father said it wasn't finished. The paintbrushes were soaking in a large jar of turpentine near the empty paint cans. I could smell the fumes from across the churchyard.

Our church was long and narrow, with two sets of steep wooden stairs leading to the main entrance in the center. There was another doorway, with a single set of stairs, that had been the women's entrance for years until my grandfather Franks became leader and told his wife and daughters to walk with him through the main entrance. Once, when I was very little, I was in church and somehow let go of my mother's hand. I remember running up and down the center aisle of the crowded church, lost, screaming and sobbing. Grandfather Franks picked me up. He wiped my tears with the rolled-back cuff of his shirt. I clung to his gray, scratchy beard and peered out at the crowd. That's all I remember of that grandfather, and Grandmother Franks had died before I was born.

No longer was the church so big. The aisle seemed short and the ceiling low. Wistfully I longed for my grandfather's protective embrace. A coldness, a scary watchfulness, moved through the room. We were gathering in the thick of it.

Everyone stared at Mother and the rest of us when we came through the door. Calmly Mother seated us in the back row, closer to the center. She kept her back to the door and instructed us to do the same. People still stared. I felt it. Father went to the front to sit with the other men.

"Hezekiel saved the Brammlett baby's life last night. Not many leaders would brave a storm like that to go get medicine," Mrs. Randolph said. She had always hated my mother for no reason, even when they were little girls, Mother said.

Mother leaned forward and said loudly to us, in the direction of Mrs. Randolph's bulbous nose, "Your father's grandfather Heart, when he was leader, built all of these benches by hand. The legs were carved and held with pegs. When *my* father was leader of the colony, he made the bottom of the benches even stronger, with metal plates. There would be no church, if not for my family and your father's."

A few heads twisted in the row ahead of us, meddlers listening and waiting, but Mother had nothing more to say.

I found myself investigating Eric's strange appearance as he sat next to his new mother. Mrs. Randolph smiled at him proudly every time someone walked past and nodded to them. Eric had to sit in the back with the women and children until he was a properly baptized member of our church. But I think the back of the church was where he wanted to be. He didn't seem too happy. Did all the boys in the outside world frown like that when nobody was looking? There was a tiny hole in his earlobe, too. The back of his neck had been shaved, probably right before moving to our colony a couple of weeks before. Had he been in jail?

All at once, a stale, warm rush of wind hit my face. Hezekiel swooped in from the main doorway and sailed past us down the aisle. Whirling around to the pulpit, he was full of angry glory.

"This is the day a strong show of faith is sought by God. It is a time of righteousness, an hour of punishment." There was a small, bloody bandage across his nose and a bruise on his cheek. Nearly everyone stared in admiration and sympathy.

The shunning ceremony. I leaned forward curiously, breathing in the fear and apprehension that slipped from the others. Naomi Schumpert glanced back at us sympathetically. Naomi's grandmother, Granny

Abraham, sat next to her and shifted uneasily on the bench in front of me. Instead of leaning forward like everybody else, she went backward. Her round, hunched back pressed hard into my knees. Hezekiel motioned for the crowd to be silent. Then he spoke again. "It is our duty, as Mennonites, to follow the scriptures exactly as they stand in the Bible. There are no other rules or laws, not of man, not of government. We answer only to God."

Old Mrs. Goode nodded and murmured. She raised her hands slightly into the air. Hezekiel glanced warningly in her direction. No one was to interrupt his performance.

"According to Apostle Paul, One Corinthians, Chapter Five, Verse Eleven, we are not to keep company, nor eat with—we are to put away from ourselves that wicked person. If I, Hezekiel Whittenstone, were wicked, you would have to put away from me. But I am not that wicked person."

The room grew quieter. Hezekiel gradually positioned himself in the familiar stance of all his raging hellfire sermons. First he crouched while leaning forward. I always feared he would really pounce one day and knock us from our benches.

One hand slowly lifted, then poised high above his head. Two fingers curled like a big claw. I couldn't look away. The claw always held me.

"Lila Franks Whittenstone has forsaken God!"

Stomp! He moved forward with the left foot and then, *stomp,* once more quickly with the right.

"Lila Whittenstone has turned her back on Heart

Colony. She gives us only one choice. She is no longer welcome in our lives. She is not to be spoken of. She is not to possess our thoughts. Drive her from your minds!"

Mother winced and closed her eyes tightly. She shook her head and opened her eyes again. Reaching for Rachel, she cuddled her protectively.

"She didn't love God. She didn't love her husband. She didn't love her children. Her sins are too many to atone for. From this day forth she no longer exists, nor ever existed! She is to be shunned. Forever."

All of Aunt Lila's children sat impassively behind the men of the church. A sob wrenched out of Mother, and my cousin Mary Helen did the most awful thing. She turned from her seat in the fourth row and stared at my mother in disgust. My stomach flip-flopped.

Hezekiel motioned to his children. My boy cousins, dreading what was to come, woefully went to stand beside him. Mary Helen sauntered over, her head proud, a smile on her face.

"I no longer have a mother," the boys mumbled, in their order of height: Daniel, Moses, Elijah, Michael, James, Peter, Noah, and Isaiah, the littlest.

Hezekiel reached out to pat each of them on the head. They shrank from his touch. Each boy shuffled back to their bench. They never looked up.

The littlest one's feet pulled up from his too-large shoes as he walked dutifully behind the others. I watched the tiny heels and ankles and wished Hezekiel had not kept our families apart. Isaiah was just a baby.

I wanted to hold him and tell him it would all turn out fine one day. He would see his mother.

"I never *had* a mother," Mary Helen said, standing there, commanding our attention for so long that I thought a sermon would soon issue forth. Perhaps Hezekiel feared the same, for he shoved her toward the benches.

"They are without a mother, and I no longer have a wife." With a bowed head Hezekiel declared himself spiritually divorced and set us free from his performance, as well. As we stumbled outside I couldn't get over how the beauty of the day did not blend well with the ugliness I had just witnessed inside.

My boy cousins avoided the pious crowd. Mary Helen pranced back and forth, grinning and bragging. She hugged Old Mrs. Goode and put on a big show that there were so many who would choose to be her next mother, how was a girl to advise her father on such things? Now and then, Mary Helen would seek out her father, to let him know of these offerings.

But he didn't listen to her at all. He stood with the crowd of men, but his thoughts clearly were on the woman waiting patiently nearby, the widow Beth Jacobs. After every few words he spoke, Hezekiel glanced in her direction.

Beth Jacobs's dress was too tight in noticeable places, and her brown hair was piled high on her head, propped up by something underneath. She felt the stares of the other women and backed away slightly. Hezekiel moved toward her.

"She is 'too sick' for church most Sundays," Mother

said coldly. "I'm glad she's well enough to attend today."

"Let Hezekiel have her," said Naomi Schumpert. "It will make it that much better for Lila."

Mother nodded gratefully to her friends. It was easier to bear Mary Helen's prancing now that I knew Aunt Lila was still in our hearts. Hezekiel's claw had not snatched that out of us.

"We want to thank you, Brother Hezekiel, for saving our baby," Mr. Brammlett shouted across the churchyard, although Hezekiel was standing right beside Mr. Brammlett and his wife.

"Thank you for risking your life to go get the medicine," Mrs. Brammlett said very loudly, and held up the baby for Hezekiel's inspection. Then she in turn inspected the tiny bandage on Hezekiel's nose and fussed over it with much enthusiasm. Others looked on sympathetically.

Joshua Mueller, with his parents, passed somberly by. A large red lump swelled tight over one eye, and there was a large makeshift bandage across his forehead, covering the wound from Hezekiel's hoe blade. Nobody gave sympathy. Everybody averted their eyes, except me.

Joshua looked away from me so fast that I couldn't stop my hurt feelings from showing all over my face. He turned back quickly enough to catch them all, even though I jerked my head down. Didn't Joshua like me anymore?

Joshua's mother had stopped and whispered something in Mother's ear. Thinking they, too, had seen my actions, I waited for the giggles, but they directed angry gazes at Beth Jacobs instead.

"Because he sent for her and she came from a different colony, I suppose," Joshua's mother was saying. "She never works the fields, and sometimes he sends the younger ones to clean her house."

"I'm glad the government wouldn't let her be the teacher. She isn't certified," Mother said. "James Ackerman was very upset when Hezekiel hired her after he'd already hired Mrs. Monroe. But that's not the real reason Hezekiel sent for her. I think he had been visiting her at the other colony. He sure left this one a lot until she moved here."

"But there is no proof of anything," Naomi Schumpert gently reminded her. "And remember what they are saying about Lila and the truck driver."

Mary Helen was easing toward us. She pretended to be smiling at Joshua, but I knew she was spying on Mother. It was suddenly clear why all these years Mary Helen had been allowed to come to our house although her brothers had not.

"They seen Lila in SlapEasy yesterday." Joshua's mother whispered, not seeing Mary Helen approach. "She's a janitor for SlapEasy High School."

Mother's eyes widened, and then she looked at me. I now knew for certain we were going to that county spelling bee in SlapEasy. And I knew why.

"Joshua, I heard you saw Beth Jacobs and Hezekiel together," Naomi Schumpert said. "Tell us what you saw. I want to hear only the truth. You know it's a serious thing to accuse without proof."

Joshua looked up and right into the face of the eagerly waiting Mary Helen. He touched the bandage on his forehead. "I didn't see nothing," he mumbled.

"That's what I thought," Naomi said. "It's very bad of you to lie, Joshua."

He looked at Naomi with a puzzled expression, then took several steps backward away from her and accidentally ended up right next to me. Before I could say anything to him, Mary Helen inched in right between us. Joshua's mother hurried away, Joshua following closely behind.

"Joshua," Mary Helen called, chasing after him.

I watched, angry and envious. She chased him past the church and under the shade of the big oak tree.

Something she said made him stop abruptly and turn around. As he walked toward her, I stood there wishing it was me. There was a strange look on his face. Maybe that was love. But how could he love her after all she'd done?

His hands reached out to her, and she was smiling the biggest smile. Something was put into her hands, and she screamed. Whatever it was jumped out, or she slung it out, I'm not sure which. I just remember being glad that wasn't me striking out at him and losing my balance and overturning the jar of paint thinner all over my dress as I fell to the ground. No, that wasn't me. It was Mary Helen's well-deserved dishonor.

5

I DIPPED DOWN to the wet shirts in the basket. Then I stood up and reached for the clothespins. Over and over I repeated this process. Read a word from the list, bend over, pick up, clip another shirt to the line. Looking up at the afternoon sun, I spelled the word aloud.

"Accommodate...a-c-c-o-m-m-o-d-a-t-e."

A newly pinned shirt slapped me with its soapy fragrance. Pulling the shirt away from my face, I held up my arms a moment longer, letting the breeze ripple through the ventilation holes in my dress. I had ripped another half inch from the seam since the time Mary Helen saw it. There was no one to see it now. Ever since Aunt Lila's shunning, Mother had had to do the harder field work with the men, instead of working with the women, but she planned the final triumph.

She'd come home each day dusty and sunburned,

her work bonnet hanging off her neck, drenched with sweat, and ask how far I was with my spelling list. She'd greet Father on the front porch and ask if anyone else mentioned his being the new leader. Then she'd lean her head against his shoulder, and if he thought none of us was looking, Father would kiss her on top of her head.

How different it would be if Father were the leader. It would be like the old days, when there was more trade with town and we didn't have to do *everything* for the colony. We wouldn't be as tired, and Mother would be running the house again. I longed for that day. I dropped the leftover pins in the basket.

"Rachel, I'm throooooooough. Come get the basket."

I know I yelled it loudly enough, and I repeated myself several times, but Rachel did not appear. So busy cleaning the inside of the house, she must not have heard me. I pulled the spelling list from the clothesline and left the empty basket by the back door.

In the middle of the yard was a raised concrete mound. Below it was the old well-water pump. I sat down beside it and waited until I was very certain no one was in sight.

Hidden inside the hole of the well cover were secrets from the school, so secret even Mrs. Monroe didn't know about them. Thanks to the swiping hands of Adam and Eli, the school no longer had a stapler or a cellophane tape dispenser. I had rescued the items from my brothers on behalf of Mrs. Monroe and the school, but never could bring myself to return them. I wondered if she had noticed how red my face was when she gave me the spelling papers and said she couldn't find her stapler. It was a wonder Mother hadn't noticed.

Pulling out the stapler, I marveled again at its mechanical intelligence. Holding it in my hand, I felt as authoritative and powerful as Mrs. Monroe. The shiny steel was heavy and everything around it reflected in the gleaming sides.

Click. I shot a metal staple into the air. *Click-click-click-click-click,* I began stapling all around the edge of my spelling list.

I panicked suddenly. If anyone saw me sitting and playing, all of the colony would condemn my laziness. I put the stapler back into its hiding place and tore two long strands of tape off the dispenser. With tape extending and floating off my hand like ghostly fingernails, I fetched the hoe from the side of the house. Wrapping the spelling list around the handle, I secured it with the tape.

The hoe cut into the soil harder than I expected. Grains of dirt flew upward, cutting into my eyes. I blinked forcefully, then wiped at my stinging eyes with the hem of my dress. Turning the handle of the hoe sideways, I read the first word tearfully.

"Mississippi!"

I looked away and spelled. "M-i-s-s-i-s-s-i-p-p-i."

Chop, chop, spell.

"Secretary!"

"S-e-c-r-e-t-a-r-y."

Several hard-stalk weeds clung stubbornly to the ground. I struck vigorously into the soil, digging down into the roots, bringing up brown, slimy worms. Throwing the hoe aside, I got on my hands and knees and yanked at the weeds close to the roots.

"Ow!" Tumbling backward, I pulled only a few broken stems with me. I stood again, brushed the dirt off my hands and skirt, and reached for the hoe.

"Impossible. I-m-p-o-s-s-i—"

"Sarah Ruth!"

Caught red-handed, I dropped the hoe. Father was standing behind me. I waited for his anger about the spelling practice.

A group of men were entering the back door of our house. Five, I counted, including Joshua's father, dark like Joshua, and Naomi Schumpert's husband, so blond his hair and eyebrows had no color. The dirt of the fields clung to the knees and the bottoms of their overalls. Samuel Lawrence, the one who tended sick livestock and administered medicines to the households when Hezekiel wasn't playing God, stared for a long moment at me, then at Father. I didn't care for him. He was much too old. And a lot of those animals in his care died. I didn't want him ever tending after *me.*

"You're a young woman," Father said. "And you'll be wanting a husband in the near future. Don't stand around talking to yourself."

I nodded and tried to quiet my pounding heart.

Father must not have noticed the spelling list taped to the hoe.

As soon as the back door shut behind him, I ripped the paper off and dropped it onto the ground. I weighed it down with a rock. The meeting at my father's house could mean only one thing. Very soon he would become the leader.

"Chrysanthemum!" I proclaimed loudly. "C-h-r-y—"

"Practicing your spelling for school?" James Ackerman stood beside me, smiling gently. He had the kindest, wisest brown eyes.

"Yes, sir." I blushed.

"We're going to make sure you can keep on going to school." He patted me on the head. "But for now, until we can get your father in as the new leader, you need to be careful."

"Yes, sir. I'm really trying."

"Now, you go practice those spelling words where nobody else can hear you." He picked the spelling list off the ground and handed it to me. "Say, you got any more of this clear tape?"

I thought hard about it. Mr. Ackerman was a very nice man and wanted to help me stay in school. It would be wrong to lie to him and say no.

"I have more clear tape," I answered truthfully, "but it doesn't belong to me."

I ran for the sanctuary of the food cellar with my spelling list.

"Chrysanthemum." I tried again. "C-h-r-y-s-a-n—"

Something scuttled between the food barrels in the

back of the cellar. A potato thudded to the dirt floor and rolled toward me.

Standing very still, I tried to follow the path of the scuttling by moving just my eyes. I wasn't sure what was in there with me. It seemed to come from the far corner, where the shallow roof sloped into the ground outside.

"It must be rats or mice," I said aloud. Adam and Eli would have to catch some of the wild barn cats and turn them loose in here.

I thought I heard a small clicking sound. *Rats, because of the claws*—I shuddered—*or because they were chewing on something with fast, busy little teeth that liked ripping into anything that moved, like bare feet.*

"Chrysanthemum—c—h—r—y—s—a—n—t—h—e—mum—!"

A small barrel pushed over and seed corn poured out onto the floor.

I shrieked and jumped backward. "Who's in here?"

"It must be rats or mice."

I heard my own voice, coming not from me—but from the corner of the food cellar!

My heart raced wildly. I remembered Hezekiel's sermon in which he told how he fought the Devil, who mocked him in the corncrib. I tingled. I shook. I spit out nervous drool, but somewhere deep inside me, I found the courage of God.

"Be gone!" I commanded. "Devil, be gone from the food cellar!"

My throat was dry. I longed to yell for Father.

Everything started happening so fast. Baskets flew to the floor, barrels tipped over, and this enormous pale force hurled itself at me, screaming.

"Stop it! Stop it! Stop talking about the Devil! You're scaring me!" Rachel nearly knocked me down. She threw the tape recorder at me. "The Devil is in there! I didn't know it. I tried to make the music come out, like you did. Oh, do you think it's the Devil?"

I smiled, much relieved, although my lips were still shaking from the scare. So that's where my voice had come from. *The tape recorder not only plays music, it keeps voices.*

"Show me what buttons you pushed to make it do that, Rachel."

"No!" Rachel screamed hysterically. She scrambled out of my grasp and ran out of the food cellar, possibly to tell someone else about the Devil box. I wasn't too worried, because the only one Rachel ever told things to was Mother. Still, I would need to keep this tape recorder concealed, since Mother thought I had given it back to Mrs. Monroe. Grabbing one of the small baskets off the floor, I wedged the recorder in, then hurried from the food cellar and plucked tomatoes off the vine so fast I bent some of the vine stems. Placing the tomatoes into the basket, I thought wisely that if I could learn to put my voice on the machine, I could call out all my spelling words to myself. Mrs. Monroe would have to show me how to do that, so I had a good excuse to go to school, should Mother catch me. Besides, Mrs. Monroe would want to know about the meeting at our house.

I ran to the gravel road that led to the south end of the colony, where cows grazed in the pastureland bordering the school. I ran past the gray, tumbling barn my grandfather Heart had built, with its white running roses peeking out between the latticework sides and doors. I loved that little curve in the road with the lattice barn and the bent-over oak that lightning had shaped. Even though my grandparents were no longer alive, I could feel them there in the sweetness of the land. On the next dirt road would be the school. Mrs. Monroe would be there, working as usual, even without any students.

6

I WAS WRONG. Mrs. Monroe's car wasn't at the school building. Small streaks of sweat stuck the back of my dress to my skin as I tried to decide what to do. I could go to the latticework barn and wait for Mrs. Monroe to come to school. That was not an unpleasant idea. I looked back at the barn. Green vines had rooted between the diamond-shaped openings and reached gracefully upward among the roses. It was peaceful there. I thought suddenly of Joshua, who had played in that barn years ago with me and my brothers. Grandfather Heart had given us a pony, and we taught it to trot around bales of hay in a pattern, only it wouldn't let any of us ride. Not that Joshua didn't try, and sprained his arm badly enough for Grandmother Heart to fashion a sling for him.

I laughed at this memory and turned to go. A wasp

suddenly popped against my neck, then flew into my face. I swatted awkwardly, overturning my basket. The tomatoes spilled out into the road.

Looking down at the orange clumps lying in the dirty gravel, I had an inspiring thought. The tape recorder was still in my basket. So what if Mrs. Monroe wasn't here? Maybe I could work the buttons by myself and figure it out.

The first button clicked, then stopped. I pushed the second button and heard my terrified, tiny voice. "It must be rats or mice."

The third button wouldn't hold when pressed down. The fourth moved the tape inside the clear window many times faster, but no sound came out. The fifth button did the same thing as the fourth but the tape ran in the opposite direction.

It would have to be the third button. I tried forcing it to stay pushed in.

Lifting the basket to my face, I talked into the recorder. "My name is Sarah Ruth Heart, and I'm going to the county spelling bee."

I pressed the second button and waited for my proud announcement. Instead I heard, "It must be rats or mice."

I frowned, then it occurred to me. I had already passed the section of the tape that held my new words. When I pressed the fourth button, the tape ran backward. It stopped. I pushed the PLAY button again. Nothing but a *shhhhhh-shush-shing* and then, "It must be rats or mice."

I was beginning to hate the sound of my own voice, especially when it was something foolish being repeated and there was no controlling it. But I couldn't give up. Sweat ran down the sides of my face, and I wiped it with my hands. I forced the third button again. My fingers slipped and also jammed the second button. Surprisingly, both buttons stayed in and the tape inside kept moving in the right direction, at the right speed.

"My name is Sarah Ruth Heart," I said again. I lowered the basket. I knew exactly the right buttons to press now.

"My name is Sarah Ruth Heart," the machine said back to me. I threw back my head and laughed real loud. I had done it!

"Good afternoon, Sarah Ruth."

Joshua appeared from behind the pecan tree just off the road and caught me with my foolish mouth still wide-open. Where had he been? In the lattice barn?

"You don't watch nothing going on around you. I could have been somebody else."

"I saw you coming toward me." I bent down and began stacking bruised tomatoes on top of the tape recorder.

"Ain't no good now." He watched me curiously.

"They can still be used, to make relish or maybe put in with the peppers." My hands shook. Had he seen the tape recorder?

"I saw you talking to your basket."

Nervously, I looked up, but kept feeling for tomatoes and dropping them in. As he moved closer to me, I noticed his left eyelid was drooping badly. The cut from Hezekiel's hoe blade started above that eye and slashed blackish red across Joshua's handsome forehead.

"They say I've been doing odd things, too." One shoulder sloped lower than the other. Joshua tucked his hand inside the bib of his overalls. "Can't remember what I'm supposed to." He tapped at his head. "Remember better than last week, though."

I felt sorry for him but didn't know what to say. I stood up and smiled. He smiled but regarded me suspiciously.

"Thought you couldn't go to school no more," Joshua continued.

"I'm not going to school. I'm taking these tomatoes to Widow Jacobs."

"I ain't telling, if that's what you're worryin' about. It's your business if you want to go to school."

"I'm not worried." I began walking toward the field of weeds behind the schoolhouse.

He followed. "Curious, you choosing to go to Widow Jacobs's. Want me to go with you?"

"Yes." I wondered if he ever got enough nerve to steal a kiss from a girl while walking.

I would never find out. No matter how much I slowed down, he never caught up. I marched through the sticky weeds, pretending indeed this was where I intended to go, but all the way I dreaded it.

The Jacobs house loomed before me. What if she

was home? Reaching the cleared-off backyard, Joshua stopped. He crouched down beside a fence post in the middle of thickly wound wisteria vines.

The dirt road in front of Beth Jacobs's house was as deserted as the schoolhouse road. I slowly approached the back door and decided to give her only two tomatoes should she answer. If Mother found out I had given her anything at all, I would never be forgiven.

Selecting two of the smallest and most squished, I spread my fingers awkwardly to hold them with one hand, while reaching up to knock with the other. Voices drifted through an open window on the side of the house. Hezekiel. There was no mistaking the cold sleekness of his voice. Instinctively, I pulled my hand back.

Without looking behind me I was aware Joshua was still watching. I pretended to be going to the front door, but as I turned the corner of the building, I sneaked in closer to the window and the wall. Joshua could no longer see me.

Hezekiel and Beth Jacobs were seated together at an ugly gray linoleum table in the kitchen, their backs to me. Widow Jacobs had her hair down! I almost gasped out loud. Hezekiel moved his hand toward her head and gently grasped the silken curls between his fingers.

"In a few days," I heard Hezekiel say, "God will send a sign showing everyone that I am the chosen leader. It will be like a miracle."

A rock hit my foot, then another. I peered around

the corner and saw Joshua, waving to me frantically. He had moved into the backyard.

I crept away from the corner of the house and toward him, but I just kept thinking about poor Aunt Lila. The anger swelled up inside me until it burst forth, wild with frustration. I gave Widow Jacobs those two tomatoes. They sailed through the open window and one must have hit her, for she cried out and grabbed at her dress. The other splattered heavily against the inside wall, leaving orange-red globs of pulp streaking down the clean, white wood.

"Go!" Joshua shoved me toward the weeds of the back field. "Get down."

Obediently I ran, and a trail of tomatoes fell out of my basket behind me. Weeds snapped and tugged at my ankles as the recorder jiggled heavily in the basket. I could hear a door open and shut at Beth Jacobs's house.

"I see you!" I heard Hezekiel shout, and I was chilled to my feet. I ran even faster.

It wasn't until I stood panting in the shadows of the school building that I realized Joshua must have run the other way.

7

I FEARED HEZEKIEL would somehow trace the tomatoes to our backyard and come pounding on our front door. He did come over the next day, but it was to invite us to a picnic. The colony needed some happiness, he said. Mother stared at him suspiciously.

The meadow by the creek held a slight cooling breeze and a perfect picnic sun. The tables were laden with lemon tarts, German chocolate cakes, cold cucumber salads, and corn-bread dressing. For once everyone was pleasant, even Mrs. Randolph, who passed the potato salad politely to my mother. The Brammletts' baby lay cooing on a quilt under the oak tree. Hezekiel picked up the baby and kissed the top of her head, where the white downy hair stuck out in all directions. The cut on Hezekiel's nose had healed, but Mrs. Brammlett worried over him.

Joshua was there with his parents, but he didn't eat.

His face still deeply marked by the hoe, he sulked among the creek bushes and sometimes didn't answer when his mother called to him.

Hezekiel's sons stood with their backs to the creek and recited Bible verses endlessly, one by one. Everyone smiled and nodded at their new religious enthusiasm.

"Hezekiel says this picnic is a thank-you from God," my father said in a low voice to Mother. "The supplies got to the colony in South America, and they sent a thank-you letter."

Mother smiled. "I'd like to see that letter."

"It's over there, on the table. It has a foreign postmark. He really did send the food there. I looked at that letter carefully."

I smiled. My canning abilities had saved some lives! I felt grown up, bigger. Perhaps I should have put my name on the bottoms of the jars so people in the South America colony would know who I was.

Mother shrugged. "I'm sure there's more behind this South America project than he is telling."

Father handed her his empty plate. "Stop being so suspicious of everything. A man who does *some* wrongs does not do *all* wrongs."

"He knows there are those who would prefer to see you as leader. He is up to something sneaky. It's on his face. I see it."

I watched silently with Mother as Hezekiel moved from group to group, patting people on the shoulder and smiling as they ate more food. "Yes, eat up," he told them. "We have worked hard. We should enjoy ourselves."

Father walked over to a group of young men who were pitching baseball. That, too, was a surprise, like the picnic. Hezekiel was allowing games again! I wondered who had hidden the baseball all this time.

"Come on." Mother pulled me along with her to a gathering of women near the creek bank. "Hezekiel asked Granny Abraham to lead the singing."

"He is allowing singing?" I stumbled after my mother. When we passed the picnic table, I scooped up a tad of pepper jelly with my finger.

"I will not lead the singing." Granny Abraham remained seated on the sagging bench that had been pulled away from the table.

"I hope whoever told on us last time for our secret singing said we did a good job," Old Mrs. Goode said. She walked crookedly over to the bench and placed a gnarled hand on Granny Abraham's shoulder. *"I got this joy, full-of-glory joy...,"* old Mrs. Goode sang in a voice more crooked than her walk.

"Joy of Abraham and Mo-ses...," the rest of the women joined in nervously. I looked up at Mother. She was singing. I looked down at Granny Abraham.

"He yelled at me for having a singing meeting the other day." Granny Abraham stubbornly kept her mouth shut during the rest of the song.

Mother reached out and lovingly smoothed down the messed-up hair of Hezekiel's littlest son, Isaiah. He darted away quickly, hiding behind his big brother. Daniel patted him on the head and pushed him back into the Bible-reciting line.

Mary Helen was eating her third piece of chocolate

cake and decided to savor the last of the dark frosting while standing by me.

"Joshua can't join the picnic because he threw tomatoes at Mrs. Jacobs's house," she said.

I glared at her bravely. "He didn't do it. *I* did."

I waited for her to run and tell everyone, but she didn't. She went back for another piece of cake. I waited for Hezekiel's sign from God, but that didn't happen, either.

"So how is school?" Mary Helen came back over to me with a sly grin and wiped the cake crumbs off her mouth.

I was ready for her. "Oh, I learned how to spell all kinds of words. Calories...c-a-l-o-r-i-e-s." I glanced at her pudgy waist.

"What about *over*?" Mary Helen asked. "School is o-v-e-r. Forever."

"Nonsense...n-o-n-s-e-n-s-e."

"Oh, absolutely over. A-b-s-o-u-l-u-t-e-l-y."

"Misspelled. Stupidity and obesity." I was really getting into this spell-off. "M-i-s-s-p-e-l-l—"

"Oh, what do I care? My father got rid of my mother for good, now that he found out where she is in SlapEasy, thanks to me, and soon he'll get rid of you. I'll be *so glad*." She gave me a hard shove and upset me so badly, I ran for home.

I WAS SITTING there by the well cover, clutching the stapler in my hand and sobbing, when Joshua sat down beside me.

"That wasn't nice of Mary Helen, even if she is your cousin."

"She's not kin to me. There's not a drop of Aunt Lila's blood in her. She must have been carved straight out of Hezekiel's insides."

Joshua gazed at me keenly, then looked down at the stapler. "That's really nice. Where'd you get it?"

"Eli gave it to me." I couldn't look up. "It's for when I'm a schoolteacher."

Joshua reached out to touch the stapler.

"You can hold it." I quickly handed it to him.

He held it up in the air and admired the silver sides that gleamed in the sunlight. Then he placed it back in my hand. For just a second his hand held on to mine. My heart felt as if it had been stapled clean through.

"I really like you," he said, and then he leaped up, tripped over the well cover, and was gone. Now I had another good reason for keeping the stapler. Joshua had touched it. I put it back in its hiding place carefully, so as not to lose his hand smudges.

AFTER THE PICNIC life went on with its usual toil in the house and fields, though I worried endlessly that Hezekiel had really found where Aunt Lila lived, just like Mary Helen said. But Mother insisted he would not kill her even if he did find her.

Every evening, after returning from the fields, Mother collapsed across the green cot in the corner of the kitchen. Her swollen feet soaked in a bucket of hot water and strong salts. Some nights she could barely walk up the stairs to her bedroom because her feet were so swollen. Father rubbed her back and consoled her that soon there would be a new leader.

Today I wished that new leader had arrived much sooner, before this shipment of denim overalls appeared with more hard work for Mother. Mother had kinfolk in the Mennonite colony outside of Memphis, though I'd never met them. Once a year boxes of partially assembled overalls arrived from that colony. Mother attached the strap buckles, cut the leg lengths, and hemmed the heavy denim. Then she turned the finished product over to the church. Hezekiel provided the list of those deserving the overalls, based more upon loyalty to him than need. Usually our family was not on the receiving list.

Mother never complained, but I suspected she hated that sewing for many reasons, especially the Hezekiel one. I hated mending, just for the tedious act all by itself. I sat there on the edge of the porch and felt the afternoon slipping away from me, so easily and so unfairly. I had asked to help with the overalls, but Mother said no, I had to mend our shirts. The shirts were easier than the overalls, according to my mother. But I didn't believe that. The shirts were a heavy weight of cotton and I had to push the needle really hard. The stubby needle pierced through a double shirt cuff, poking into my callused thumb tip. It left an indentation, although I couldn't feel it for the numbness. I hated turning shirt cuffs. Take a worn-out shirt, turn the collar and the cuff inside out, and it was supposed to be like new again. But it wasn't.

Anyone could tell it was an inside-out, frayed cuff. It would be faster to sew on new cuffs. This job didn't make a whole lot of sense. And it wasn't fun to have little holes in your thumb and first finger, or to be going blind from picking out tiny little stitches all day long. But what would they do with the old cuffs if we just made new ones? Nothing was ever thrown away at Heart Colony. Everything was used and reused. An ugly possibility came to me. Quilts! Made from old shirt collars and cuffs. Even more sewing and suffering. It was better to keep one's ideas about mending to oneself.

The backs of my knees were sweating. That's what I didn't like about our long skirts; there wasn't any way to make it cooler underneath. I tried inventing ways, but modesty mostly prevents my saying how. I moved to the lower front step and stretched my legs straight out, letting my skirt fall away from my legs. Reaching lazily for the patch basket, I accidentally dropped the needle into the full dress gathers of my lap.

Clang! Ding, ding, clang! The fire bell! Jumping up, I shook my skirt until the needle dropped to the bare dirt. I picked it up and tossed it into the sewing basket, then ran toward the road. I left shirts and cuffs scattered on the porch steps, but I didn't care.

People were running from all directions, from the houses, from the fields. The bell rang faster. The afternoon clicked from slow motion to fast, as everything moved into a solemn rush. The water truck cranked up in the distance, backfired noisily, then died out. It cranked again, then rumbled loudly. I could see the dull gray tank moving down the road away from our house. I followed the direction of everyone's panic.

White smoke spread out low in the sky over the next hill. Darker puffs pushed under it. I smelled the fire, strong and sickening-sweet, reminding me of the early summer burn-off of poisonous vines from the yards.

"Naomi's house." Mother was suddenly beside me, her hands grimy with field dirt. We ran like the others until we were close enough to see the flames.

There was an awful wailing from far down the road. Naomi Shumpert, arms stretched outward, yelled and screamed at everyone she ran past.

"What is she saying?" I shouted. My eyes were stinging from the heat and bits of fire swirling all around us in the smoke.

"I can't hear her," Mother shouted back. Everyone was screaming and yelling. The noisy water truck arrived. Father ran along behind it. He was so brave. I watched proudly. He yelled at the men to grab buckets off the truck, then shouted angrily when they discovered there were no buckets on the side of the tank.

Naomi came screaming to us, pulling at her dress bodice as though she was going to rip it off. She clutched at her heart and screamed again. "Granny Abraham! Granny Abraham!" She pointed to the house.

My blood ran cold, freezing up into a big chunk in the middle of my heart. I looked at Mother and then at the house. Huge flames were twisting around the back and creeping steadily to gulp up the sides. Naomi's husband was wrestling a fire-damaged white cabinet off the porch. He could not hear.

"Solomon!" Mother yelled through cupped hands.

My father didn't hear, either. He stood by the big dent in the water tank and tried to fit an irrigation hose from the fields into the side opening. *Where is the regular hose to the water tank?* I wondered.

"Solomon!" Mother screamed again. He turned toward her.

"Granny Abraham is in there!"

There was a deadly silence as everyone realized what was happening. Naomi plunged headlong toward the fiery house but was caught by Mother. Father and the men moved cautiously toward the house, glancing at each other in silent reasoning. I didn't want my father to go in there. He might not ever come back out. Mother looked away. I could tell she was crying.

Strangely, no one had to go in. For at that moment Hezekiel appeared from inside the burning house. He carried Naomi's frail grandmother in his arms. Black smoke billowed out from behind them, coating the trees and porch with lingering streaks of black powder. The crowd gasped admiringly as Hezekiel pushed through it all. Naomi fell to her knees in thankful prayer. Hezekiel strode proudly off the porch as though the fire could not hurt him, although the flames seemed to be caught on the back of his heels. Granny Abraham was wheezing and coughing. He gently placed her on the ground beside Naomi. Naomi clutched at his knees and sobbed her eternal gratitude to her leader and hero. The fire roared and crackled, enveloping everything in its path.

There were loud pops as windows burst and glass shattered, warning us to move back. The crowd moved into Joshua's yard across the road. I kept watching for him. I guessed him to be in his room, possibly looking down at me. Waves of heat pulsed now from within the fire. The water truck was being backed into Joshua's yard. The truck then stopped, and Mr. Caroll got out. He motioned frantically to Hezekiel.

"My house, my house," Naomi sobbed, standing there watching desperately. Granny Abraham was laid out on Joshua's front porch. Some women were fanning her face. Joshua's mother brought her a glass of iced tea.

"Where are the buckets?" Hezekiel demanded of my father, coughing hoarsely. "Where is the fire hose?"

"I don't know." Father was bewildered.

"It is your duty to see they stay on the truck," I heard Mr. Caroll say.

The flames rose higher, clinging to the outline of the fireplace. I watched, fascinated. I had never seen brick carry a fire before.

The back wall of the house was bending, and the side facing the road began to blacken. It finally collapsed into the older flames hugging the center foundation.

"Get the boys," Hezekiel yelled at Mary Helen, who appeared as if on cue. "Tell them to find the buckets and hurry."

I felt so sorry for my father. It was obvious he blamed himself for the catastrophe. Mary Helen took off running, and I hated her, even if she was my cousin, just for the way she was holding up her skirts.

Dark smoke from the fire filled my lungs, cutting off my breath. I moved back further and opened my mouth wide, gasping at all the clean air around me. The inside of my nose clogged with soot. Some people held handkerchiefs over their noses.

Joshua's father came outside of his house and handed my father a bucket. "It's all I could find."

Hezekiel wrenched it from Father. "This has to be done right, or we'll lose more houses."

The other men murmured in agreement and listened as their leader explained how they could contain the fire. Father stood there by the water truck, staring at the empty hooks where the buckets should have been. James Ackerman walked by and reassured Father it wasn't his fault.

My boy cousins appeared shortly. Each of them carried two buckets, except for Isaiah, who could only manage one. Daniel, the oldest, nodded to me as I stepped out of the way. He stayed by the water tank with Father and held the irrigation hose over the buckets to be filled.

The men ran with the buckets and began drenching the grass surrounding the house. Then they began closing in on the fire, sloshing water into the larger ring, making the fire press inward and upward, until it leaped across at them from another side, chasing them away. Father kept filling buckets and in between that tried to stretch the irrigation hose toward the fire and water down what he could. Slowly, though, the fire came under control. There wasn't much left to burn. The panic was over. The big black blanket of smoke was floating away into the sky.

"At my cousin Amelia's," I heard my mother say to the rest of the women, "they baked pies and cakes and sold them every day in the nearby towns. In less than two years, they were able to buy a used fire truck that the men could repair."

I sat by the road and began to wonder, as the rest of the men ran around with reddened faces and singed beards, how this fire had been so calmly and well met by Hezekiel.

Mary Helen was not a swift runner, not with that body. How did she find her brothers so fast? Once she found the boys, the buckets would have to be fetched from the large supply barn, a good distance away. Not only did the boys arrive too quickly, their actions were so strangely rehearsed.

Naomi Schumpert was crying again. I turned my head just a little, so as not to shame her by staring. She was sitting on the ground, clothing and cooking pans and canned jars of vegetables planted in caring little rows around her by all the women of the colony who passed by.

"This quilt I cannot take," Naomi said, wiping the tears off her face with the corner of the double-ring blue-and-white coverlet. "This was your mother's wedding quilt, Mary Helen!"

"Take it," Mary Helen said, shoving it once again to

her. "The scriptures say we must give unselfishly to one another."

My mother moved away sadly from the gathering of women. The mere sight of the quilt greatly pained her. *How did Mary Helen get that quilt here so fast?* I wondered.

Children laughed and chased one another as evening slowly descended. The Schumpert house beams lay in a heap, glowing softly like giant fireflies in the smoky darkness. The men patrolled around the embers, while the women gathered in a little closer and talked quietly. The odor of wet ashes and melted plastic reminded us the excitement was almost over. It was time to go back to the chores and vigorous routine of life and be thankful. But I couldn't stop the questions that ran through my head.

The water truck started up again and drove closer to the dying fire, illuminating the sad ruins. Naomi's husband paced back and forth, leaning over piles of treasured rubbish and poking a big stick around. He was very angry, and suddenly he pointed the stick up at Hezekiel's throat. I couldn't hear what he told him.

"You can't be sure," Hezekiel said loudly, getting the attention of the crowd.

"I am sure." Mr. Schumpert stood there poised to lop off the head of anyone who came near. "Somebody set this fire."

Everyone around me gasped, then moved in closer. Mother was watching Hezekiel but was more concerned with the sad figure of my father.

"Go get my shovel," Mr. Schumpert ordered the boys waiting restlessly nearby. He pointed to the small shed in the backyard corner that had been spared from the fire. My cousin Daniel took off running to it.

"I will dig out the proof of this fire," Mr. Schumpert said, pointing to a specially selected pile of ashes. "Why haven't you got my shovel?"

"The door won't open," Daniel yelled. He had one foot on the door frame as he pulled with all his might at the latch.

Mr. Schumpert cut through the glare of the water truck's headlights to get to the shed. His wide shoulders swung at an angle as he thrust all of his weight against the door.

The shed door opened and Joshua ran out, his clothes soaked with sweat, his dark hair matted down. I breathed in so fast, it hurt my ribs. I didn't understand this at all. Neither did Mr. Schumpert.

"What are you doing here, boy?"

Joshua backed away slowly and fearfully, blinded by the truck headlights. He tried to see who was standing beyond the lights, then, open-mouthed, realized there was a crowd.

Daniel said something to the other men, and then Mr. Schumpert peered into the shed. He motioned for the other men to hurry forward. Hezekiel was the first to go in. He came back out and held up a metal container and a small box.

"Fuel and matches," Hezekiel called out to the crowd.

"I've never kept anything like that in this shed." Mr. Schumpert shook his head.

"Please!" Joshua's mother screeched as she ran into the path of the headlights and kneeled. "Have mercy! He doesn't know what he's doing. He can't help it. Ever since the beating—"

"Why would you burn my house?" Naomi Schumpert pleaded to Joshua.

"You called him a liar, didn't you?" Hezekiel said sternly. "He accused me of having an affair with Widow Jacobs, and you called him a liar. It made him very mad at you. Mary Helen told me."

The crowd murmured angrily as Naomi agreed that was true.

"He burned down my house." Mr. Schumpert raised his fist, his voice trembling.

Hezekiel dropped the fuel can and reached for a shovel, raising the blade high into the air. "Come here, boy."

Joshua ran, his feet flying out clumsily. We could hear the stinging of weeds and the tearing of thorns as he disappeared into the field. The running footsteps rushed the dried grass and thudded on toward the woods just past the creek.

Hezekiel stood there with the shovel still raised, but no one chased after Joshua. My heart was zipping around inside me like lightning.

"He threw tomatoes at Beth Jacobs's house." I heard one of the women behind me say.

"They say he was proud to admit it."

I wanted to scream at them that Joshua was innocent of the tomatoes, but I sat there guiltily with my heart still zipping and my mind whirling. What if Joshua really was the one who started the fire?

"I accept responsibility for my son," Joshua's father said heavily. "I will see that he is punished."

"Will you see that he brings back my house?" Mr. Schumpert asked angrily.

"Please don't beat him again." Joshua's mother kept her thick hands folded in a permanent pleading.

Hezekiel lowered the shovel and then raised his claw hand at Joshua's mother and father, sending them back across the road. I could hear Mrs. Mueller crying and screaming to God as she went inside her house.

The crowd slowly left. The water truck started up, putting the scene of destruction in a kinder cloak of darkness.

"STAY WITH US." Mother leaned over to her best friend and patted her shoulder reassuringly.

"No," Naomi said, shrugging off Mother's hand. "We choose to move in with the Moteses."

Mother stiffened but pretended this didn't bother her.

Mr. Schumpert was standing in the dim light of a lantern, opening and shutting the damaged drawers of the small white cabinet. The drawers were empty. The back of the cabinet had a huge burned-out hole.

I turned and hurried ahead of my family so that I could pick up the shirts and cuffs left strewn about the porch steps. I hoped I could collect them all in the dark.

"Goodness!" Mother bumped into the box of overalls on the porch. "I need to sort these."

I was sent into the house to turn on all the lights and search the kitchen for leftovers.

Father came into the kitchen and rinsed all the black streaks off his arms and face. "I've lost the right to become leader. I don't know how I forgot to put those buckets on the truck."

"Only *you* think you've lost the right." Mother comforted him, walking into the room. She handed him a towel and rinsed the sink out.

"No, it's in the eyes of the others, as well. Hezekiel offered Brother Schumpert his job back as manager of the colony office. He's going to take it, he says. Remember when he quit, it was to show support for me, to join our side, but now—now he questions my leadership value."

"You didn't start the fire. That boy did."

"Because of me we couldn't end the fire." Father threw down the towel. "Hezekiel was the real leader today. It was very clear. To everyone."

It was true. Everyone once on Father's side had been snatched to Hezekiel's bidding during the fire.

Mother looked at me sadly. I knew what was coming but didn't want to hear it. When Father left the room, Mother gently reminded me to bring in the clothes and said to forget about the spelling bee in SlapEasy.

I flipped the yard-light switch and concentrated on getting the clothes off the line. I couldn't rage or cry. Disappointment overwhelmed me. I reached up to grab a pair of overalls. There was a rustling sound in the weeds and then a flash of blue denim. For a moment I thought the overalls had slipped off the line and were running away from me. I lunged to catch them, despite the ridiculous thought, then saw bare feet running along with them.

"Good-bye." The husky whisper belonged to Joshua. A yellow flower plunked through the air and hit me on the arm—at about the same time it hit me that the role of "leader," made so very clear to everyone during the fire, could have been Hezekiel's planned "sign from God."

8

LUMPY WHITE GRITS lay splattered across the cabinets and the kitchen floor. All of us looked up from the breakfast table. This was so unlike Mother, to waste food and show fury.

"No!" Mother picked up another plate from the counter. "I won't go."

Father stood there in his gray Sunday shirt and pants and stared down at the grits. "You have to go."

"*You* go, and you sit with those who are no longer our friends. I will not do such. I'm sick of it." Mother angled the plate so that scrambled eggs slid off and landed on the floor by the grits. Crumbling the bacon in her hands, she let it fall, too. I had never seen her act this way.

"You want to let them treat you like a dog, then I guess you want me to treat you like a dog, too. There's your breakfast."

"Enough! Come to your senses!"

"I have." Mother's shoulders were heaving up and down. "Who do they think they are, coming over here and telling me what I have to ask God's forgiveness for? My father was a good leader, and I won't stand for that talk against him. I won't stand for that talk against *you*."

"This only makes more talk."

"Now Hezekiel wants to tear down that barn. Your father built that barn for your mother's flowers. How can latticework be sinful? It was to allow air, and a little shade, not for show. Hezekiel is jealous of the name Heart, and all of us bearing it. I won't stand for it! Not anymore."

I stared down at my plate. I wasn't sure if it was safe to continue eating.

"Get ready for church," Father shouted at all of us. Adam, Eli, and Rachel scooted their chairs away from the table and ran from the room. I moved just a little bit slower.

"Hezekiel's going to say bad things about your father today in church," Mother called angrily. "You don't have to go if you don't want to."

"The children are going. You don't know if what you are saying will happen."

"They said you will be chastised for trying to be leader, and for the buckets and fire hose being gone from the truck."

"I deserve to be called on it. It is the way of our church."

Mother shook her head. "It's not the way our

church used to be, and you are a man of God. I will not sit there and have you called otherwise."

Father smiled, grateful for her loyalty, but then his face became sternly set. "Please, we have to do like everyone else. I cannot stay hidden in my house. A full day has passed since the fire. I must go to church, and I expect my family to go with me."

"I'm staying here with Mother." I spoke before she could change her mind.

Father pressed his thumbs into the sides of his head, stroking upward to the temples. I could see he had a bad headache building.

"Next Sunday you *will* go, both of you. If anyone asks today, I won't lie."

While the children dressed for church, Mother waited in the front parlor with me. She kept staring at the box of overalls, and I guessed she was worrying over the big sewing task awaiting her. When my brothers and sister came downstairs, they were reluctant to come into the parlor. Mother called to them calmly.

"It's fine now. Everything will be better."

She buttoned the top of Rachel's dress, then gave a warning to my brothers not to wiggle about during the sermon. Father opened the front door and left without speaking to us. The little ones hurried behind.

I could tell Adam had on the wrong shirt, for when he waved good-bye to us from the porch, his arm wallowed in yards of gray cloth. Too late I realized he was wearing one of the shirts from the mending basket. It was missing the right cuff. If I called him back to change, it might further anger Father and make all of them late for church. Adam shouldn't have been in my mending basket, anyway.

"IT IS TRUE about Hezekiel and Beth Jacobs," I said as Mother scooted the huge box of overalls out from the corner of the room.

"What proof have you?"

"I heard them talking."

"It's a sin to eavesdrop. Are you sure it was them?"

"I saw them."

Mother raised up wearily. "*You* saw them, or you're repeating what Joshua supposedly said?"

"*I* saw them. Hezekiel was in her house. Her bun was undone, and his hands were in her hair."

Mother winced. "Sarah Ruth, if you are making this up, I will whip you within an inch of your life."

"The window was open, and I heard him say that soon he would do a miracle. There would be a sign from God to the colony that he was meant to be our leader."

"What will be his miracle?" Mother asked. "His message from God? He doesn't need it now that the fire—"

She stopped and her eyes widened.

I nodded. I reminded her how my cousins arrived so soon with the buckets and how Hezekiel, who should have been in the fields, was passing by the Schumpert home exactly when the fire started, so that he could go in and rescue Granny Abraham.

"It's simple then." Using opened-out scissors,

Mother sliced through the cardboard flaps of the big box. "We must get proof. Nobody is going to take your word for it, nor mine, nor your father's. And then I think what we should do is go to another Mennonite colony, one that follows our way of thinking, not Hezekiel's. Here, I want to show you something."

Digging deep into the box, she began pulling out unfinished overalls and stacking them on the floor. With each pair she opened them out and felt the pockets. At last she smiled and held a pair of overalls up for me to see.

The pocket had been sewn shut.

"My cousin Amelia buys these from a factory because they're flawed. Their colony makes money selling clothing and other supplies to other colonies. She and I used to play together, when my father was the leader and everyone was allowed to visit other places.

"Then, as we got older, we used to write to each other, but when Hezekiel took over, we couldn't use the mail service anymore because it was a part of the U.S. government. He didn't want us to talk about other colonies, either."

"Mrs. Monroe was right? We're not like other Mennonites?"

Mother nodded. "On some things. Hezekiel's interpretation of God's will is sometimes confused with Hezekiel's right to *be* God. I don't think he knows the difference. Not too many people around here do. I'm lucky. My cousin Amelia sends me letters in the clothing supplies, and when I get to sell vegetables in town,

I mail letters to her. So I know what it is like in other Mennonite colonies. I know what it *should* be like here."

"Could I read some of the letters?" I asked, fully expecting her to say yes.

"No," Mother said simply. "I've had to destroy them soon after reading them so no one would find out."

I felt so honored being the only person Mother trusted to tell about Cousin Amelia's letters.

"I think we're twice different from other Mennonites," Mother said. "Because first, we're in the South and it's already so different from the rest of the United States, and second, we have a leader who isn't like other Mennonite leaders."

She stacked the overalls back in the box. "All this time I had been planning with Cousin Amelia for us to move to her colony, should I ever convince your father to leave. But now I see what really must be done. Hezekiel must be stopped. He set that fire. What I don't understand is, why was Joshua in that shed?"

She sent me to Joshua's house to find out. His family would not be at church, we guessed.

I stepped outside thinking that two roads over, at church, imprisoned worshipers were watching Hezekiel's claw and being stifled with odd body odors. It didn't bother me that I roamed freely over fresh-scented clover and they could not. If only all my Sundays could be spent like this. Surely God understood.

I did not feel as joyful when I passed the Schumperts' crumbled home. A charred coverlet lay on the scorched ground nearby. The stench of the fire could still be inhaled.

I crossed the road and knocked shyly on the Muellers' door. I hoped Joshua knew I was sorry he took the blame for my tomatoes, and Hezekiel's fire. Today I was the messenger of hope and truth for him. He really needed to talk to me. I knocked louder.

Joshua's mother and father came to the door. Their usual smiles for me had been replaced by cold stares and anxious glances between them. I asked to speak to Joshua, but they ignored me. I studied where my skirt hem was rubbing the black soot from the road onto my feet and asked again.

"It's really important."

"Joshua can't come out." His father closed the door. Joshua would have no visitors. That must have been what the good-bye the other night meant.

"I have to ask him something important. I can help." I tried sliding my words through the crack of the door. It was no use.

Walking backward from the door, I hoped to see him wave from an upstairs window or to find a yellow flower discreetly tossed my way. But all the windows upstairs had been covered with the heavy gray broadcloth used for Sunday shirts. I gave up and went home.

FATHER WAS ANGRY when he came back from church.

"Sarah Ruth has not been tending to her chores. That is how it looked to God and the others who saw her brother's Sunday shirt without a cuff."

"We will not argue over a full table and empty stomachs." Mother sat down and immediately passed the plate of buttered corn halves to Eli. "Let's eat."

"School did that to her," Father said, sitting down. "She doesn't know anymore what is important in life."

"Hezekiel has seen the Devil take over animals' and people's bodies, changing them from good to evil," Eli said excitedly. "He told us about it."

"They care not to hear about church today." Father silenced him.

"Somebody's getting a little too big for their britches," my mother said, glancing first at Eli. Then she took a long, hard look at my father. "And somebody else is getting a little too biblical for their britches."

He left the room.

The change in the colony was changing my father. In the old days he might have joked about the shirt, asking if his son had grown a shorter arm. Or he might have asked me, How did this happen? It didn't matter. I knew what was really important in life. That spelling bee I was being denied was worth more than the thousand future shirts I was destined to mend.

That night I stood in the bedroom and pretended Joshua was in the yard, watching as I took down my hair. I could feel he was out there. As I leaned out the window and stared into the night, I saw a flicker of light at the creek. In six more days, on Saturday, I thought, the county-wide spelling bee would be just as much a lost dream to me as Joshua was now.

9

I'LL NEVER KNOW what made me get up so early that crisp Saturday morning and dress in the dark. I was suddenly going to that spelling bee, and I was going in my best blue dress. I moved as if by no choice of my own. Four times it took before I could tighten my hair into a bun. I felt like a stranger creeping downstairs and slipping out the back door. My breath all hushed and choked—*Hurry, hurry*, the tightness in my stomach warned me. A silvery trail streaked across the wet grass behind me as I left the safety of my yard for the freedom of my dream. Once the sun came out and dried the dew, my family wouldn't be able to see what direction I'd taken, but unfortunately most of my family was up and working long before the sun.

I took Aunt Lila's path through the rows of damp soil and healthy crops. Always watching behind me, I was nearly dizzy from the constant turning around while hurrying forward. At last I slipped out of the fields, away from Heart Colony's main road and onto the highway to SlapEasy.

I hesitated. What if something happened to me and my family never knew? But Aunt Lila had made it safely. And what if I was caught? James Ackerman would support me. He was still in a position of power at the colony, despite the recent upheaval and the stronger support shown to Hezekiel. James Ackerman wanted me to go to this spelling bee, I assured myself.

Determined, I continued onward. A creamy yellow sun floated up over Heart Colony and its milk white buildings. If I were an outsider viewing the colony from this distance, I would find the place harmonious and ruled by God; but if I were an outsider, I might not hear the voice of God.

The loud muffler of a car scared me off the road long before I actually saw it.

The brown mud-dauber station wagon. *Hezekiel!* I began running along the side of the road. There was no escape. Barbwire fences blocked the fields on both sides. The car was swerving closer. I leaped off the road into tall weeds and rusting cans. I lay low in the damp ditch and panted in terror. The car jerked from one side of the road to another, searching for me. It pulled even with my hiding place, then passed, braked, and whirred angrily as it backed up. I lay there praying my faith would make me invisible.

"Get out of that ditch!"

It was my mother! I looked up and gratefully realized she was alone. I could win this one.

I stood up. "I'm going to the spelling bee, and you can't stop me."

My dress was soaked around the knees with ditch water.

"Get in the car. I'll take you there."

I was much too smart for that. "No. I want to walk."

Mother shook her head. She didn't appear angry, but I couldn't be sure. "Don't you know how long it takes to walk to SlapEasy from here? Most of the day."

"Then I'll run."

"Then that's your choice." Mother started up the car and drove ahead of me. Lifting my skirts, I ran as fast as I could but not fast enough. My run gradually changed into a brisk walk, with her slowing down the car to watch me. The sun grew stronger and my legs weaker. I was dragging into a half crawl. By the time the ditch water dried on my dress, I had given up. Almost.

"Stop!" I screamed, waving frantically.

"Now are you ready to ride?"

I perched on the hood of the car and held on.

My mother refused to drive. "You'll fall off and get squashed on the highway."

I refused to jump off. She blew the car horn, and I ignored it.

She got out of the car and shook her finger in my face. "You think I won't take you to SlapEasy? I don't lie. I said I'd take you, now get in. You're wasting time.

The spelling bee will be over by the time you get through throwing fits. If Hezekiel and Beth Jacobs can sneak off, we can, too."

I got in but crawled over the backseats to the very end of the station wagon, where there was a lever to open the back gate to get out.

"Why are there melons back here?" There wasn't much room for me to sit, unless I wanted to sit on that mound of chains that Hezekiel used to secure the car when it was parked.

"I put them there. When I realized what you had done, I told the boys and Rachel I was selling melons in town with you today and to tell your father."

It occurred to me she might have expected me to do this all along. She clenched the steering wheel and tried to make the car go faster, but it wiggled and shook a lot harder. We were all over the road. I think my mother had driven a car only one time before.

"Don't sit there dreaming out the window. Spell your words."

"I can't." I pushed a heavy melon out of my way. Who could think of spelling words while trapped in a tilting car?

"Hezekiel has ruined this car. Look how everything keeps going the wrong way and won't stop."

We drove for miles. Farmland was soon chopped up into fenced lots with smaller, one-story houses. A bait shop with rows of fishing poles against its window looked deserted. A small cemetery with cracked white stones was littered with large cedar limbs, broken about. Then the road curved wickedly. We passed a Stop-and-Smile gas-and-food store, its orange metal signs welcoming all travelers.

As we entered the SlapEasy city limits, Mother got better control of the car. I didn't feel so in danger.

WELCOME TO SLAPEASY was spelled out in white rocks on a small hill. Bushes with tiny red leaves formed a square around the message, and blue plastic whirlybirds had been stuck in the ground all along the bushes. I held my breath. What an exciting place!

What would the school be like? The town had squeezed-together stores in red and brown brick. The big plate-glass windows caught our reflection as we drove past. How shiny all the other cars were! No one else had a painted-over car like ours.

Mother had broken into a sweat. "I don't know where the school is."

"Let's ask." I crawled over the backseat, making my way toward the front. "Pull in there—"

Mother slammed on the brakes, sending me sprawling to the floor. She turned the wheel a little at a time and slowly managed to angle the car into a Better-Bagging grocery store lot. The back tire bumped over something, then the car crashed downward, jarring my teeth so that I bit my tongue.

"It was part of the sidewalk," Mother said, opening the door and peering out to see. I jumped out from the backseat, grateful to be on the ground.

"I'll go ask that man." I smoothed my dress and tried to cross the parking lot, but Mother grabbed my sleeve.

"No! You wait for a woman. You don't go up to strange men."

He didn't look so harmful. His dark hair was short, and his white shirtsleeves were whacked off at the elbow so that his arms looked too long for him. He didn't notice us and went on into the store.

A woman pulled up in a tiny black car, and she stepped out wearing a long black shirt and no pants.

"I'll ask her, then." I tried to move, but my sleeve was still pinned to the car-window ledge.

"No," Mother said. "Look at her black-and-yellow hair. She's a very bad woman, you can see all of her legs."

I think the woman heard us, but she smiled at me, anyway. I thought her hair was interesting.

"There—go ask them, those children." Mother pointed to three girls coming out of the store and pushed me in that direction. I didn't like the girls. They had a hateful look in their eyes. Their dresses were nearly as long as mine, but not as full, and of lighter, brighter pastel prints. One was yellow, one pink, and one blue. All of them had their hair in buns, like mine, but each had the bun covered with a black net, and even had several twists of curls across the forehead. The sleeves of the dresses were cut off at the elbow. All the people in Slap-Easy, it seemed, liked to show off their arms.

"Could you tell me, where is the school?"

The middle girl, in the pink dress, started to speak, but the older girl poked her to be quiet. They stared at me impolitely for a moment, then lifted their heads haughtily and walked away.

"Please," I called after them. "I have to find the school. I'm in the spelling bee!"

The girls turned around. One stuck out her tongue at me. The other held up a small black book and shook it at me. I think it was a Bible.

"The school is two streets from here. Turn left at the next corner. Go straight. You'll see it."

The man my mother hadn't wanted me to speak to was being polite enough to help. I held my hand against my face so Mother could not see my lips moving.

"Are those girls in the spelling bee?" I asked worriedly. "Will there be more like them at the school?"

"Oh, no." The man laughed. "They go to a private school. But not everybody at their school is like that."

He put coins into a large metal box and pulled out a newspaper. The metal door slammed shut. We used to read newspapers in Mrs. Monroe's classroom, until Hezekiel found out. I wanted a newspaper now, to show Mother, but I had no money.

"Hey! What colony are you from?" the man suddenly called after me. I could not answer. I was in full view of my mother.

When I returned to the brown station wagon, she was frantic. "What did you say to him? You *know* not to speak."

"He told me where the school was. He was being nice. Those girls were mean. They reminded me of Mary Helen."

Mother tried turning left at the next corner, stopping traffic for a long time. Car horns honked. People shouted out the windows. As we were finishing the turn, we were startled by the windshield wipers and all kinds of blinking lights.

"*Thank you,* Hezekiel," Mother said, flinging her hands up into the air.

I didn't like Hezekiel, either, but I really felt Mother held the responsibility for this mechanical madness.

She gave me the impossible job of finding the right control switches to turn everything off, which is why, when we pulled up to the school, everyone was staring at our car. That, and the fact that our car resembled a mud-dauber's nest and didn't have a lick of shiny.

Cars were parked all along the sides of the street. It was a big crowd. I was suddenly frightened.

"I don't believe I want to do a spelling bee," I said.

"I believe you will." Mother got out of the car and slammed the door shut. She held the other door open for me. Reluctantly I stepped out into the street. Our car would have been easy to spot even without the ugly paint on it. It was the only car parked half across the road, at a different angle from the rest.

People stood on the spacious concrete steps of the school and stared curiously at us as we walked up. Children were running to swings and shouting happily. I stared up at the three-storied brown brick building with its white concrete columns and wished, just for one day, I could go to a school like this.

At the top of the stairs were four huge arched doors. We stepped inside the main hall. The auditorium could be seen through glass panels. It was just like Mrs. Monroe had described it. She said it was an old school and SlapEasy badly needed a new one, but to me, this was a beautiful place with shiny wood floors and tall graceful ceilings. The stage that we would stand on had dark blue curtains draped across like an early night sky.

Girls walked by with soft, flowing hair and short, perky dresses. I noticed something else, too. Everyone around me, boys and girls, had on shoes. In my haste to sneak out of the house, I had forgotten mine. I was suddenly thankful for my very long dress.

Mother got up the courage to ask another mother where the rest room was and pulled me along with her. "I'm not going in there by myself," she said.

The bathroom was for girls only, and girls were inside spraying their hair with stuff that smelled like it came out of a crop duster and made it hard to breathe.

"Would you kindly stop?" Mother asked.

They sprayed the air even thicker, then ran out of there giggling. Despite the room's sticky fog, I found something interesting.

"Don't be staring. You'll make yourself vain." Mother pulled me away from the mirror over the sink. "Stand right over here. Don't move."

She went into the small partitioned area where the commode was and shut the wooden door. I could see her feet below but knew she couldn't see mine. I moved back to the mirror.

My hands flew to my head and jerked out the bobby

pins. My freed hair hung loosely, but it didn't softly sway or curl. It was straight, lifeless, and had nearly a thousand bobby-pin kinks. My face was prettier, though. I could tell right away that if mirrors ever came to Heart Colony, my vanity would keep me busy.

I decided to see what my legs would look like if my dress were shorter. Bending down, I grabbed the bottom of my skirt and turned it under as high as I dared, almost to my knees. I tried to secure it all around the edges with bobby pins, but the pins were not holding too well. The commode flushed. The stall door creaked open, and Mother screamed.

"Shame!"

She plucked the bobby pins from my dress hem, tossing them all over the bathroom floor. At least I didn't have to worry about her sticking them back into my hair, not after they had landed on that dirty tile floor. Besides, she was so angry about my legs, she didn't notice my hair.

She fussed me out of the door and down the hallway. "Words I didn't understand, and nasty words, written on all the walls, and you pulling your dress higher, and all those mirrors, just a den of iniquity, a den of sin." Mother was never going in a school bathroom again for the rest of her life.

A woman motioned for us to come to the small table in the lobby. "Aren't you in the spelling bee?" she asked.

I nodded my head, but Mother stared suspiciously. "We're not sure yet."

"Are you Sarah Ruth Heart, from the Mennonite school?"

Again I nodded. My mother's face turned white.

"Nobody is supposed to know we're here," she leaned over and whispered.

"Mrs. Monroe told me. It will be all right." The woman smiled pleasantly. She pinned a green paper circle on my dress. The number 37 was written in the circle with gold glitter. "We're so glad you came."

"No one must know," Mother said fearfully.

"I understand," the woman said, not looking at us anymore. "Go sit on the stage, Sarah, and your mother can go in the auditorium to watch you."

"How did that woman know it was you?" Mother held the door open to the auditorium. Her hands were shaking.

"Mother, we're the only Mennonites in this building."

"Oh." Mother glanced down at her long brown dress thoughtfully.

We entered the auditorium, where voices echoed in the big open spaces. Parents were sitting restlessly in narrow wooden chairs that connected in rows. I counted over twenty-five rows, then I counted hairstyles puffing out from all the ladies' heads. A little boy threw his milk bottle to the floor, then cried, grasping out his hands as it rolled away. Mother sat down by the outside aisle and nodded for me to keep walking.

The floor slanted downward as I made my way to the front. My legs shook as I climbed the stairs by the side of the stage. I felt everyone watching me. I crossed the stage and sat down on a warped metal folding chair. The girl beside me smiled.

She had brown skin, and one green eye and one brown. Her dark hair was cut short and curled in tiny twists all over. When she smiled, big dimples added to the unusual features of her face. I immediately liked her.

"I'm Cassie. I go to SlapEasy School, and you have the longest hair I've ever seen. Where are you from?"

"I'm from—" I felt guilty and ashamed. The words *Heart Colony* wouldn't come out. I looked down at my dress and, to my further embarrassment, noticed dark grass stains and streaks of mud showing up clearly under the bright lights of the stage.

"All spellers report up here, please." It was the man who had given me directions at BetterBagging. He wore a black coat over the short-sleeve white shirt and dark pants of a thin material that matched the jacket.

Children were hurrying up the stairs to the stage. I waved to my mother, like the other kids were doing. Mother sat forward as though in church and motioned for me to stop. She glanced around nervously. Satisfied I had not drawn too much attention to myself, she relaxed a little and stopped clutching the wooden armrests between the seats.

Some of the mothers were holding up big black tape-recorder things, and children on the stage were making faces at them. I didn't think Cassie's mother was out there, because Cassie wasn't acting a fool like these others.

Mrs. Monroe walked into the auditorium and sat

down. Her sleek white dress and simple pearl necklace caught Mother's attention, although Mother tried not to look. I waved to Mrs. Monroe. Mother frowned.

The spellers beside me were wiggling and squirming so much you could hear the dented metal chair seats popping. My heart was ready to leap off the stage and race down the aisle, dragging me with it. Every seat in the auditorium was filled, and people were standing up in the back.

"We will now start the practice round," a thin woman with short gray hair and white chunky legs announced. "Stand."

I did everything Cassie did, except instead of staring out at the people, I kept watching the announcer. Those legs didn't look right under that narrow, red-striped dress.

"First row, move to the front of the stage. Approach the microphone one at a time, in the order of your number. We will begin now. Number one, step over to the microphone, please."

I panicked. What was a microphone? I leaned forward and glimpsed a short little boy with a number-1 circle pinned to his shirt. He was standing in front of what I saw must be the microphone, a tall metal pipe.

"Bubble," the woman said.

"Bubble. B-u-b-b-l-e."

When I heard how loud the little boy's voice was, I understood what a microphone did. Now I had two things to worry about—spelling the word correctly and speaking into the microphone.

The other spellers moved swiftly ahead of me, spelling their words and returning to their seats on the stage.

"Number thirty-seven."

I walked across the stage with my glitter number and freed hair and reached up for the microphone. I was scared to touch it because of the electric wire.

"Bicycle," the woman said to me.

Fear gripped me. Every word was now in a foreign language, and all I could think about was that a thousand people were probably seeing the ventilation rips under my arms. I pressed my arms downward slowly and tried to think of the spelling word. What had it been? It was an easy word. Bubble. Barbecue. Bicycle. That was the word. Bicycle. *Spell it,* I scolded myself. Everyone was leaning forward now, urging me to say *something* and get out of there.

"Bicycle," I said breathlessly, my voice ringing out across the auditorium.

A woman standing in the very back turned and looked up at me, astonished. It was Aunt Lila! Thin and with a ghostly color to her face! She held a large push broom and was cleaning the back of the auditorium, by the glass panels. So Mary Helen was wrong! Hezekiel did not get her.

"Time is running out," the announcer with the chunky legs said.

"B—y— Oh! No!" I realized my mistake too late, while blurting it out. The audience sighed in sympathy. I headed for the steps off the stage and kept my head down.

"Number thirty-seven...young lady...come back here. This is the practice round."

I felt even more stupid. Slinking low, I found my chair on the stage again and fanned myself with the green circle that had been pinned to my dress. Glitter came off and stuck to my sweaty hands.

"That happened to me last year," Cassie whispered. "Only I kept on going down the steps and out of the auditorium."

The first round proved to be difficult. Half of the spellers missed their words and were sent back out into the audience. I stood there trembling and slowly spelled my word. "Ingenuity. I-n-g-e-n-u-i-t–y."

"Correct," the announcer said. She never smiled.

The second round knocked out even more of the competition. I knew it was wrong to smile because someone else messed up, but it felt so good to be among the ones who didn't.

On the third round Cassie missed her word. This time I did not smile. My only friend was leaving the stage. She wasn't sad, though. She was grinning and waving her hand good-bye to everyone.

"I protest," a woman said, jumping up from the audience.

Cassie stopped on the stairs and dramatically groaned. The auditorium became hushed. A dark-complected, attractive woman in bright red pants and jacket walked up to the stage and made the announcer run the tape recorder back. Until then, I didn't know we were being recorded.

"There!" she said triumphantly, as the three all bent over the machine, listening. "You hear that? The word was not pronounced correctly. Cassie spelled what was pronounced."

The man in the dark suit apologized, but the announcer in the red-striped dress was mad. They made Cassie go back to the stage.

"Sometimes I hate her," Cassie sighed, flopping down beside me.

"Is she your teacher?"

"She's my mother *and* she's a teacher. Kind of a bad combination, isn't it? I don't want to be here. She made me come, and I could have been modeling fashion clothes instead."

More contestants missed their words and I did mine right. It was Cassie's turn.

"Congregation," the woman said to Cassie.

I couldn't believe what an easy word they gave her. Maybe it was because she was a teacher's child and her mother had stood up and complained.

"Congregation," Cassie said loudly. "K-a-h-n-g-r-a-g-a-i-y-s-h-u-h-n-n-e."

She used so many unnecessary letters, I lost count of them. Her mother, in the front row, visibly cringed, then stormed out of the auditorium.

"See you later," Cassie said gleefully. "I've got to be in a fashion show."

She merrily skipped off the stage, and I bravely looked out across the audience for Aunt Lila's face.

Now there were only five of us in the fifth round,

and then two of us in the seventh. The smart little boy with the number-1 circle wouldn't look in my direction.

"Individualism," the announcer said.

That was *my* word, my very own special word, and they gave it to *him.* I squeezed my hands together. How hot it was under those stage lights. *Hurry and spell my word,* I thought mournfully.

"Individualism," he said. "I-n-d-i-v-i-d-a-" He stopped, grunted loudly in fury, then shut his eyes.

"No," the announcer said. "That is incorrect." She shook her head at him.

He moved away from me, waiting and hoping for my mistake.

"Individualism." My bare feet stuck out from the plain Mennonite dress. With glitter sparkling on my hands, I pushed the long strands of kinked hair away from my face. "I-n-d-i-v-i-d-u-a-l-i-s-m. Individualism."

"Correct."

The noise startled me, and I stepped back as the entire audience clapped loudly. I stood there reminding myself to keep my arms down, and then I saw Aunt Lila, one row behind my mother. Mrs. Monroe was coming up the stage toward me.

All these people were talking to me. The man from the BetterBagging parking lot walked up to the microphone.

"Sarah Ruth Heart, of Heart Colony Mennonite School, is the new county spelling champion. Congratulations, Sarah."

He handed me a white envelope. "I should have known you were a Heart. You remind me of your grandfather, that same lively look about your face."

Mrs. Monroe hugged me. Bright lights flashed in my eyes, and I stumbled away from the crowd to my mother.

"What is this?" Mother was afraid to take the white envelope.

"A savings bond. It's like money, Mrs. Monroe says."

Mother peered inside it. I still clutched it tightly in my hand. "But it isn't real money?"

"It can be used like real money."

She snatched it out of my hands. "Doesn't matter how it's used. We can't take it. No, we can't."

"Hannah—" Aunt Lila was suddenly beside us and reaching toward Mother.

"I told you to go to Cousin Amelia's, where you would be with other Mennonites," Mother said angrily. "Why did you come here to live? You won't survive."

She pressed the white envelope into Aunt Lila's hands. "This is money. Use it."

Mother pushed me through the crowd before Aunt Lila could say anything more to us.

I wanted to stay and talk to all those exciting, sinful people, but Mother kept on lightly pushing me, all the way down the school's front steps and out to the colony station wagon.

"WE'LL SAY THE melons were spoiled." Mother drove the car much too fast for the narrow town streets.

I was still numb from the noisy crowd and could only watch silently as everything exciting about Slap-Easy disappeared behind us.

All the ride home I waited for her to tell me she was proud I had won. But she never did. She slowed the car down long enough for me to toss the melons out and did not speak again the rest of the way.

10

FATHER WAS WAITING for us when we pulled into Hezekiel's drive. "The melons did not sell—we had to throw them out" was all Mother offered by way of explanation of where we'd been.

"James Ackerman is dead" was all my father said, and he left us standing there wondering how.

I could not sleep that night. I thought about James Ackerman and I thought about winning the spelling bee, and I couldn't even shut my eyes.

Because she felt guilty for driving me to the spelling bee and for lying about the melons to Father, and because James Ackerman, our last big supporter, was dead, Mother missed church the next morning. I heard her arguing about it with Father. I missed church because it was no longer part of my world. I had performed, and won, in the outside world. I could not go to church. My new knowledge kept me from going. It wasn't that I was displeased with God, and I knew He understood, especially since I spent most of my Sunday morning praying in the latticework barn. The colony would always be a part of me, a part of God, but Hezekiel's church was that painful speck in God's eye that needed to be plucked out—only I didn't know how He was going to do it. I did ask that He find a way and find it quickly. I also thanked Him for letting me go to the spelling bee. I proudly prayed that James Ackerman, after he died yesterday, had somehow seen me win and that he was glad. I know it sounds blasphemous and vain, but I hoped my beloved dead grandparents, along with James Ackerman, and a host of angels all had seen that moment when the announcer said my name as the winner on that big, scary stage. But I hoped none of them had noticed my hair was down. I don't know what possessed me to cast my belief aside and fling my hair about with no shame during the spelling bee, but surely I was forgiven that little transgression.

I gloried in the secret that I had won. The voice booming inside of me wanted to shout, *I am the county spelling bee champ! I won!* But that would have been a foolish thing to do, and each time I thought like that, I prayed hard that I would return to modesty.

Modesty and humility returned soon enough, when Mother and I finished dressing for James Ackerman's church and burial service that Sunday afternoon.

"You two will stay at home." Father pointed to me and Mother. "You weren't here in the colony when he died, and you should have been. So you will stay and not show your faces with the rest of the grieving congregation."

"But—I was his favorite child on the colony!" I stepped forward to follow behind my brothers. "They didn't even like school or Mr. Ackerman." I pointed to Adam and Eli. "Why should they go and not me?"

"Sarah Ruth!" Father took a step toward me. My mother reached out and grabbed my arm in warning. Then she put her arm around me protectively.

"We will stay here and pray for James Ackerman in the house," my mother said quietly.

"Me, too," said Eli. He and Adam bolted for the back porch.

"Come back here," my father called out, then raised his eyes questioningly at my mother. "Maybe they should all stay." He nudged Rachel in the direction of my mother, then left for James Ackerman's church service on his own.

I followed a safe distance behind, Mother being too preoccupied with a scuffle between Adam and Eli to notice I was gone. But I did not go as far as the church. I watched my father follow the road, his walk more resigned than angry, then I ran across the fields to get to the burial yard behind the church, where nobody could see me.

I stood over the fresh open grave dug for James Ackerman and felt in my pocket for the spelling list I had practiced with. After wiping away a few tears, I dropped my spelling paper into the grave, then kicked in some fresh dirt to cover it. I didn't really do any hard crying until I returned home.

ON MONDAY MRS. MONROE stared at me in disbelief. I had sneaked over to school just long enough to say I wouldn't be going to the state competition. It was too far to travel without the colony noticing I was gone. Just picturing the crowd of outsiders that would be staring at me—an even bigger audience this time—frightened me. Most of all, James Ackerman was dead. The tractor had overturned, I told her, and with it went the only support left for me going to school and being in spelling bees.

"That should be the biggest reason to go. Because he would have wanted you to. If you weren't going to do all of it, you shouldn't have done any of it." Mrs. Monroe was very mad.

Holding back my anger, I assured her the boy in glasses who'd come in second and never smiled at me would be *happy* to take my place.

"Just go," Mrs. Monroe said at last. "I'm sorry I cared so much and tried so hard for any of you. You don't care, and you don't try. Do you know how that makes me feel as a teacher?"

Papers flew across her desk as she slammed the grade book down. I ran out to the quiet pasture and cried bitterly. I hated Mrs. Monroe. *She* didn't understand. She didn't even try.

FATHER SAID VERY LITTLE to me at supper, except that I should ride with him in the farm truck to the dump site. Father had been clearing off the remains of the Schumperts' burned house all day. A charred stove and several unidentifiable globs of wood and metal were stacked in the back of the truck, as well as the burnt-out white cabinet.

"They asked about you in church. You and your mother could cause trouble for all of us. That's the second time you didn't go."

So that's why he asked me. He didn't need someone to watch the back of the truck. I was along only for the lecture. I could have reminded him that he didn't *let* me and Mother go to the funeral service, but I didn't. I chose not to respond and stared out the window with the same vacant expression my mother had been using on him for the past week.

"You're going to church this Sunday." Father pulled worriedly on his beard as he talked about things God intended for us to do, all the rules of our colony—the words swam before me but did not soak in. I could only hear the audience of the spelling bee clapping louder and louder for me.

The gravel road bumped downhill. Loose gravel spun up from the tires, hitting like buckshot underneath the truck. The sun disappeared. The sky was flimsy and colorless as we backed up the truck so we could slide the stove and other debris into the slimy green water.

We got out of the truck, and a putrid splash of waste water nearly spotted my clothes. The smell of the fire still clung to the stove. I scrunched up my nose, then watched as Father tilted the small white cabinet off the truck. The empty drawers flew out, and from behind them a small charred pad of white paper fluttered into the mud by my feet.

Hezekiel Whittenstone, I glanced down and read. *SlapEasy Bank of Progress.*

Father was still struggling with the cabinet.

"Stand back," he said in warning.

As I moved away from the truck, I scooped up the pad of paper with Hezekiel's name on it and folded it into my hands. It was thick and dug into my flesh. Father stuck his hand into the big burn hole at the back of the cabinet and lifted it off the ground, then tossed it into the swamp. Thick, nasty swamp water splashed up all around the cabinet as it landed with a thud. Father walked to his side of the truck and opened the door. "Get in," he said, nodding to my door. I ripped the cardboard from the pad of paper in my hands and got in.

Everything darkened in the sky and fields as we drove away from the dump. A low twinkling of light appeared over by the creek. Father braked, peered out at the darkness, then shrugged and drove on. Seconds later I saw them—two people walking by the creek and carrying lanterns. Joshua's parents!

"Did you see that?" I asked worriedly. "What are they doing?"

They ducked behind the trees as the truck passed. No doubt it was them. Joshua's father was so tall and big-shouldered, his mother so wide in the hips that the rest of her body bobbed on top like a duck floating in water. What were they looking for? The horrible, scalding realization reached inside, scooping out my soul. They were looking in the creek for Joshua. *Oh, Lord,* I prayed. *Oh, please no.*

"I saw no one."

"Over by the creek! I think it was the Muellers."

"You worry about going to church, that's all the worrying I want to hear from you." Father cut me off.

Mother would tell me. I turned my head so I didn't have to look at Father.

TEARS ROLLED OFF the side of my face, trickling past my ear and down my neck as I cried silently that night. Poor Joshua. He never knew how much I had loved him. He had knocked Mary Helen down, hit Hezekiel with his fist, and willingly took the blame for my tomato throwing. I'd never find another love like that.

Mary Helen added to my misery the next day by appearing in our house. Just the sight of her was bad enough, but she had to open her mouth, too.

"My father says your mother better get to the fields right now."

"Mother is sick. She can't go."

"She's always sick when it comes to church or field work. If she doesn't show up today, my father is going to kick your family out of Heart Colony."

"He can't do that. He doesn't own Heart Colony, and neither do you. Besides, Beth Jacobs *never* works. We know all about Beth Jacobs. Your father can't control every*thing* or every*body*."

"He boarded up the school today. Mrs. Monroe shows up even without any students just so she can get a paycheck. He's getting rid of her, too. My father can do whatever he wants."

"The school is owned by the government. It's part of public education."

"It's on Heart Colony land, and my father's gonna tear it down. The bricks will be used to build us a new house. I wonder what I'll take from your house after you get kicked out."

She turned to leave. I shoved her so hard against the door, I could hear the splat of her fat, ugly stomach. "Your father is a wicked, evil man who hates everybody and everything, and you're just like him."

Reaching up, my cousin yanked my hair so hard, part of it came out of the bun. Some of it lay torn in her hands. It hurt so much I stood there in shock. She opened the front door and screamed from the porch, "Soon you'll see how much everybody hates *you* and *your* family. You'll have nowhere to go."

She was lying. She always lied. Nobody could be kicked out of Heart Colony. A person could be shunned but not kicked out. The government wouldn't let anyone do anything to that school building, either. They had won the last fight. The teacher had to be qualified, and no one in Heart Colony had ever finished grammar school. Then Hezekiel brought Beth Jacobs from the other colony and the government still said no, even though she had graduated from a high school. That's how we got to keep Mrs.

Monroe, whom Mr. Ackerman had hired in the first place. She'd been to college. We couldn't be kicked out of a colony that had been named for my family, and Hezekiel had no say-so in anything to do with the teacher or the building of our school. But I decided I would check, just to be sure.

The morning was nearly over. I needed to hurry. The house had not been cleaned, but Mother would want to know about the school because of the direct way it affected us. She would forgive. And she had told me to take the tape recorder back.

No one was out in the main section of the colony. I didn't have to sneak from road to road. The noon heat was settling in on the land. Everything was calm and in its place. Mary Helen had lied. I was becoming more and more certain of that, until I turned the last corner of the dirt road that led to the pastures. My heart dropped. It was true. I clutched my basket with the recorder.

Large boards were nailed across the windows and doors of the school. A huge padlock and chain stretched across the steps, blocking entrance to the building.

Mrs. Monroe, sitting on the hood of her car, stared forlornly at her imprisoned classroom. Everything Mary Helen had said might be true! Hezekiel had kicked out the teacher, and we would be kicked out of Heart Colony next. Where would we go? The only one who might be able to help us would be Mrs. Monroe.

Moving closer, I saw she had her books, the small flag, the picture frame, and the pencil can gathered up beside her on top of the car. Hezekiel must have tossed those out, to show her that she would never be coming back. I knew she would wait, though, just like she was doing now. I wondered how many days she would actually sit and wait. I had the feeling that all good teachers were very hardheaded.

There was movement several yards beyond the school. From the back fields by Widow Jacobs's house, Hezekiel emerged. In his hand was a long brown-and-black shotgun. He was headed toward the school.

Mrs. Monroe, in her straight black skirt and apple red blouse, didn't see him. She was busy brushing her fingernails with the sinful red paint that looked like so much fun.

I waved my arms and shouted, but I may as well have been a flying mule. No one expected to see me. No one looked up.

Hezekiel sneaked around the corner of the school. My heart throbbed hard enough to burst open. He raised the shotgun, and *BOOM!* I thought my heart had exploded. He shot right over Mrs. Monroe's head.

"Git out of here. Don't you ever come back to Heart Colony." He kept the shotgun aimed at her. His beard tucked itself under it.

She tumbled off the car, taking books, papers, and everything with her. The fingernail paint spilled over, leaving two big red polka dots on the shiny silver hood. Her shoe fell off in her haste to jump into the car. Frantically she opened the car door again and reached out for the shoe. Hezekiel aimed the gun lower, at her hand. She quickly slammed the door and left the shoe lying there.

The car started with a powerful roar, then backed crookedly out of the school driveway.

A second later the car was inching forward into the driveway again. Sobbing, Mrs. Monroe got out and grabbed the picture frame and the small American flag. She yelled something at Hezekiel as she tripped over scattered pencils and books, but he only laughed.

The car backed out of the driveway again. The shotgun held high over his head by the claw, Hezekiel shouted out his victory. He stood there gloating for only a few seconds before realizing Mrs. Monroe's car was speeding straight for him. The triumphant shout became a cowardly yelp as he leaped off the road, landing on crumpled legs while trying to keep the gun stable.

I wished she had hit him, but I knew Mrs. Monroe would have jerked the car out of the way if he hadn't moved. Hezekiel struggled to his feet, stumbled back out to the road, and raised the gun. I took refuge behind a tree, as the car and the shotgun were both aimed in my direction.

The car was so close I could smell the heated engine. The gunshot crackled across the peaceful pasture road. My shoulders drew up in fear as I listened for the shotgun shell to find its home.

The car kept going, slinging gravel as the tires

fought the corner to the main colony road. I don't know what Hezekiel *did* shoot. Perhaps an unlucky bird, or a squirrel, or a tree. I was afraid I'd find out it had been the tree I was hiding behind. Long after the car was gone, I waited and watched. Finally Hezekiel went back across the fields to Beth Jacobs's house.

When I came out from behind the tree, I hesitated. The urge to run home and stay put was a strong one. The image of Hezekiel aiming that gun set me to trembling. He could have, and more than likely would have, shot me, too, just for being in the way. But then, my whole family was in his way. Then I remembered my tape recorder.

11

"IF YOU REMAIN MARRIED, I will stop seeing you," Beth Jacobs said.

"I have a spiritual divorce, recognized by the church," Hezekiel answered smoothly. "What does it matter what the laws are in town?"

"Lila has been trying for a divorce, and you refuse to sign the paper. What am I supposed to make of that?"

"How do you know that?"

"I went to SlapEasy."

"To spy on me?"

"I do whatever is necessary to keep my name free from an unclean reputation."

"I forbade you to go to SlapEasy. You know that. The other women are to go to the market, not you."

Beth Jacobs laughed. "No one is going to steal me away from you, if that is what you are afraid of."

"I know only of the danger in SlapEasy. This has nothing to do with...other things."

"Love?"

"No." Hezekiel coughed nervously. "Reputations. Being with me keeps your name above question. I am sinless. I can do whatever I want and still be sinless. I have the power over this colony and everyone in it."

"You don't have any power over Lila anymore, and yet you choose to stay married to her."

"Lila owes me years more of hard work. She left me with this family that needs a mother."

"I think you must love her."

I moved closer to the wall and held the tape recorder a little higher, closer to the window.

"Her father begged me to marry her. She didn't have the faith," he said. "But her family *never* followed the ways of the colony as closely as they should have. If her father had not died so early, he would have been removed as leader."

"Then you married her because she was the leader's daughter and he asked you to."

"God chose me to be the leader. It wasn't because of whom I was married to. It was my duty to God to marry Lila."

"Then God will understand your legal divorce. Until you get one, I must ask you not to come by this house."

"I *put* you in this house."

"None of us owns anything in this colony. All of it is God's."

"Then you cannot choose who can come in or not come in this house."

"No, but I can choose to leave for another colony should this one cause me discomfort. I am not in fear or awe of you," Beth Jacobs said angrily. "You stand there and be fierce all you want, but I am not like the other women in this colony. I would slap you, should you *dare* humiliate *me.*"

"You would do no such thing. I am the leader. God forbids it."

A chair creaked, and a heavy sigh came from Hezekiel.

"Why don't you trust me?" Beth Jacobs pleaded. "Why do you only say things that are cruel and hurtful? I know there's kindness inside."

"There's nothing weak inside. I am the leader because I am strong."

"But you're so stern. The colony I came from wasn't this rigid. We could wear wristwatches, jewelry; we could laugh and play games."

"I *gave* you your picnic, if you'll remember. And you came to *this* colony because your colony is dying out. There was little food or work for you. Your leader was weak."

"You're strong." She was purring her words at him. "I am admiring of that, but if you can't share things with me that you wouldn't tell anyone else, then I have nothing more to give you."

"I stay married to Lila because she stole all the tractor money, every penny that Heart Colony entrusted me with to buy that new tractor."

"So you lied about the outside world cheating you?" Widow Jacobs was angry again.

"I couldn't tell anyone the truth, and I kept trying to make Lila confess. That's why I beat her that one time, when everyone was talking about the bruises I put on her. It wasn't my fault. She said she was keeping all the colony's money for herself and that I'd have to beat it out of her if I wanted it back. But I couldn't. She took the money with her to SlapEasy, that's why she ran away. And I'm trying to get it back. There now. No one else knows that."

"Yet you stay married to her?"

"This is a sacrifice for the colony and for you, my remaining married. I'm trying to get the money back, and if it went to court in SlapEasy, I'd need to be married to her to get at least half of it."

"How can she keep it if it isn't her money?"

"I have no proof to show which dollars are ours, and I don't know where she put it. If anyone finds out, my leadership will be in question."

"LILA WOULDN'T STEAL!" Mother angrily slapped at the tape recorder.

"*Shh!* Listen!" I moved the tape recorder out of Mother's reach. My heart was still pounding hard from the run home with this treasure.

"If she took all that money," Widow Jacobs was saying, "why is she working? I hear she has a job cleaning commodes and scrubbing floors. Why would she do that if she didn't have to? I don't believe you, and I don't know if I would marry you."

There was silence, followed by Hezekiel coughing lightly. He spoke so deliberately it was almost spooky.

"What if she didn't take the money, but if anyone finds out it's missing, we'll say she did?"

My hand went over my heart. *Poor Aunt Lila can never really escape.*

"I'm not saying I have it. But if I did, only those very close to me would ever know."

I shut off the tape recorder. "That's all of it."

"You're very brave." Mother hugged me. "You must have been very close to where they were. You weren't in her house, I hope."

"No," I said, quite honestly. "The window was open, and they were very loud."

"Hezekiel is always too loud." Mother nodded. "But this time I'm glad for it."

WHITE PAINT SPECKLING his overalls, Father came home at supper and said he wasn't eating. A special meeting had been called for the men at church. He barely had time to wash up.

"I know all about it." Mother followed him up the stairs. "It's supposed to be against us. Don't go to the meeting. Call one of your own, and Sarah Ruth and I will stand beside you and help. We have proof against Hezekiel—"

"And the Schumperts once said they had proof, and where are they now? Sitting next to Hezekiel's throne. You don't understand, do you? There is *plenty* of proof against *us*. Nobody wants to side with us at all. We have lost."

"Then let's go to one of the other colonies to live. This colony isn't like other Mennonite colonies, anyway."

"We're not like other Mennonite colonies, because *this* colony is our home." Father's paint-covered fingers pointed angrily. "I am part of this colony, and so are you. Our families built this church years before we were born. We grew up here."

"Be a man, Solomon. So what if the other men don't stand up with you? Don't cower to Hezekiel as though you were a woman."

Father moved as if to strike her. I grabbed Rachel and covered her eyes. I couldn't reach Adam or Eli. We all stood in the hallway, open-mouthed, and watched as our father turned into a Hezekiel.

"If your sister hadn't run away, if you and Sarah Ruth hadn't stopped going to church, and if you had gone to the fields to work today, *this wouldn't have happened!*"

"Yes, it would. Hezekiel wants to punish me and Lila for *his* father's death. But it wasn't my father's fault. He sent him to get parts for the old tractor, not to get killed. The outside world did that, not me and Lila. My sister didn't deserve to be beaten like a dog, and I am not a man. I will *not* do men's labor. No, not any longer." Mother climbed the stairs after Father. It looked as though *she* was going to hit *him*. I covered Rachel's eyes again.

"You caused some of this. You wanted to be the new leader. That's why Hezekiel wants to kick us out. It isn't only because of my sister, or Sarah Ruth, or me. It's because of you, too."

Father's face blackened. The bad headaches were seizing him, throttling him until his neck bulged and his eyes became bloodshot.

"Yes, then. I accept the blame, for me, for all of us!" Father shouted. "Now leave me alone. I go to the meeting for my punishment."

Mother started to say something, then stopped. Looking down the hallway, she noticed us for the first time. "Go eat!" she yelled.

We scattered to the kitchen. None of us spoke. Most of the food remained on our plates as one by one we pushed it aside. Where usually just a plate of yellow crumbs remained, slices of corn bread sat on the counter, untouched, unwanted. In the ominous quiet, we desperately tried to prove our family unity. At last, Mother came in silently and ate. Eli picked up dishes, and Adam helped me clean off the table. Rachel was having trouble breathing because of her allergies again. I put a cold cloth over her face.

Dressed in the gray Sunday clothes, a slight sunburn streaked across the tip of his nose, Father came down the stairs, ready for the evening meeting.

"Think again on what you're doing." Mother thrust something into his hands. The tape recorder! Surely he would smash it!

"What's this?" Father held it out cautiously.

"Mrs. Monroe gave it to Sarah."

Immediately Father handed it back, then purposefully wiped off his hands.

"No," Mother said determinedly. "You should listen to this. Sarah caught Hezekiel's voice on it."

She handed it to me and motioned for me to play it.

"Don't—," Father warned me. "I know what a tape recorder is. I care nothing for what might be on it."

I pushed the PLAY button and followed him with it as he tried to walk away.

"What if she didn't take the money, but if anyone finds out it's missing, we'll say she did?"

At the sound of Hezekiel's sly voice, Father turned around. He stared at the tape recorder angrily, but at least he was willing to listen.

"I'm not saying I have it. But if I did, only those very close to me would ever know."

"The tractor money?" Father asked.

FATHER TOOK THE tape recorder with him. Mother and I secretly followed in the dark, leaving the boys with Rachel to watch the house. Hezekiel's reign of terror would soon be ended. Mother and I especially wanted to see it happen.

The doors of the church were open. The light from inside illuminated the front lawn and the big oak tree at the side. God was watching us from that tree—it gave me shivers. We reverently knelt several feet away from the building, in the dark shadow of the tree, and watched for Hezekiel's doom.

Locusts shrilled high around us. I leaned forward and could see the backs of the men as they sat on the benches inside the church.

Something moved near us. I felt it passing by, and I grabbed Mother's arm. At first I thought it came from the tree, then worried that it was Hezekiel himself.

Mother's body tensed, angled to run. The dark movement neared the church and came out into the light. Joshua's parents tiptoed past the open doors of the meeting. They continued on their way to the other dark side of the churchyard and on down the road.

"What are they doing?" I whispered.

Mother replied she didn't know.

"They're searching for Joshua."

"I never said that."

"I saw Mr. and Mrs. Mueller at the creek with lanterns. Twice."

Mother sighed deeply. "Nobody knows what happened to him, Sarah Ruth."

"They think he's dead."

"Don't say what isn't there. They can't find him. It doesn't mean anything until they find him."

A low sob escaped from me just once, then I bowed my head and prayed they would not find Joshua in the creek, that he would always be alive and here at the colony.

Mother nudged me. Opening my eyes, I saw my father was standing up inside the church, the tape recorder in his hands.

"I am told you would kick me out of the church. This is a meeting about me."

"No." Deacon Randolph tugged worriedly on his long gray beard. "This is a meeting about the colony in South America."

"Why would there be a call for that?" Father took his time, staring at all of the men fully.

"They want more instruction on our ways," Mr. Schumpert said. "They admire our strict interpretations, truer to the Anabaptist movement of the old countries centuries ago."

"In time," Deacon Randolph said, "we could change *all* the Mennonite colonies to our ways."

"I see nothing wrong with the other Mennonite colonies," Father said. I could feel Mother smiling at him in the dark.

"There's nothing wrong with them," Samuel Lawrence explained, his hands outstretched toward Father as if he would push him away. "Our colony is thankful for the others, but we feel that sometime there are those who wander away from God without knowing they are."

"Such as me?" Father clenched his fist. "Such as my family?"

"Solomon Heart, you feel guilty over some wrongdoings and that is why you are here and why you suspect our innocent meeting. Guilt is what's bothering you."

I could hear Hezekiel but not see him. There were too many brown-and-red–bearded men gathered in the front three rows to distinguish him.

"I was told by a friend you wish to kick me out. You did not invite me to this meeting to talk about South America."

"Your name *was* brought up a moment ago." Deacon Motes shifted on the bench to get a better look at

Father, but remained seated. "We decided to let your family remain in church after they confess and take their punishment. Also, you must give up the German Bible you have been translating and desist telling others that our interpretation of the Bible is wrong."

"That was my grandfather Heart's Bible that he used when he was leader. It was a gift to me, and the translations were written by him. I will not give that to you. It is wrong of you to ask."

"Very well, but your family still has to confess and take their punishment."

"My family has nothing to confess."

"You plotted against God and the church." Hezekiel was rising up suddenly from the middle of the men. He pointed accusingly at Father. "Everyone has confessed against you."

"You have the colony's money hidden somewhere, the money that should have been used to buy that new tractor. It wasn't the people in SlapEasy who cheated us with fancy paperwork. It was you. I have *your* confession." Father clutched the tape recorder.

"Money hidden somewhere—" I suddenly remembered the paper I had retrieved from the cabinet. "The bank!"

"Shush!" Mother whispered, pulling me back down into the shadows. "Stay *here.*"

"But— I think I can prove where the money is hidden. I have papers from the fire—"

"Let your father handle this," Mother said, and she firmly gripped my arm.

Hezekiel was saying, "I haven't any money. Your

wife's sister took the colony's money. Everyone here knows this. Perhaps she's offered to share it with you and that is why you come forward now with false utterances."

The men nodded their heads in agreement with the leader.

"You took the money, and we have this tape of your admitting to it." Father held up the tape recorder. "You made up the story about the outsider salesman who took the tractor money and disappeared. It's all here, your voice, on this."

"We all know that because he explained it to us," Deacon Randolph admonished my father. "We know what Lila did."

Too late I remembered I had never shown Father how to turn the tape recorder on. But he was smart enough with mechanical things, he could figure it out. But he never got the chance, for Hezekiel opened up a newspaper and held it in front of Father's face. Father's fingers froze on the tape recorder buttons. He was horrified by whatever was in that newspaper.

"This is how the Devil works, so he can bring in the outside world to destroy God's kingdom here. With each little temptation we give in to, we will want a little more of that life in the outside world until what we want is to not be a Mennonite, and to not abide by God!"

Hezekiel was raising that claw hand in the air. "Look closely, Solomon. This is where your wife and daughter were when your best friend, James Ackerman, was killed. They were at a spelling bee in SlapEasy. See, there's your daughter right there. In the picture."

Mother and I gasped.

"They did not kill James Ackerman."

"No, but they had the car we needed to take him to the hospital so he could be saved."

I felt very ill. My spelling bee victory was horrible, so small and insignificant. I hated myself deeply for what I had done.

"If he hadn't been driving that old tractor—" Father began.

"We waited almost an hour for the ambulance to arrive." Hezekiel would not let up. I covered my ears but could hear myself crying. *I caused Mr. Ackerman to die?*

"If you had bought the new tractor like you were supposed to—" Father was unrelenting. "You knew the old tractor was dangerous."

"And who welded that heavy cart to the tractor hitch, causing it to be so dangerous if it tilted?"

"I did." Father's shoulders drooped as he set the tape recorder on the bench. He sat down, lifeless and defeated.

"The blood of James Ackerman is on the Heart family's hands," Hezekiel said. "Does anyone want to hear what is on this tape? Does anyone really *need* to hear it?"

"I don't want to hear it," Deacon Motes said. "I understand what Lila did, and I can see what her brother-in-law is trying to do right now!"

There were angry murmurs of agreement among the

deacons. Deacon Caroll left the bench to go stand beside Hezekiel. Soon all the men were doing the same.

"We better go." Mother was on her feet, tugging at me. "We can't let them see us out here."

"Bring your wife and daughter here tomorrow for the church decision on their punishment." I could hear Hezekiel shouting as we ran away in the dark. I could feel my head hurt and throb, just about where Joshua had his scar. But didn't I deserve it? I had caused James Ackerman to die. My feet felt leaden and my blood ran heavy with guilt. I was no good, evil, because of my vanity over spelling words. I wished I could jerk that spelling paper up out of the ground underneath poor Mr. Ackerman's casket.

"WHY DID YOU DO IT?" Father asked hollowly when he walked into the house. "Your picture in the Slap-Easy paper. Your hair down. That woman standing next to you."

I guess Mrs. Monroe was in that spelling bee picture, too.

"Why didn't you tell me?" Tears rolled down his face. "I'm not left with any choices. Tomorrow we'll all be punished."

Mother tried to touch his hand, but he moved away.

"Not if we go to another colony to live," she said. "My cousin Amelia says there's room where she is, and it's a nice colony. There are no beatings, or hatred. Some of them work in town—"

"How do you *know* this is still true in their colony?

We're not allowed to get mail without Hezekiel's approval. More secrets from you and Sarah Ruth?" He rubbed the sides of his face. The headache was taking over. "What you and Sarah Ruth did was wrong. And after you did wrong, you didn't tell me. That's much worse."

"If you're thinking we caused James Ackerman to die just because we took the car, *that's* wrong. Poor Sarah Ruth looks ill, she's so upset and has cried so hard."

Father gripped the side rail of the stairs. "What I'm thinking is that you're like your sister, trying to turn the children against our religion. Everybody talked about how Lila let the boys run wild, but now they will start saying I have a wife and daughter doing the same."

"Where is the tape recorder?" Mother asked quietly.

"Hezekiel took it. Nobody wanted to hear it because of what you and Sarah Ruth have done."

Mother watched him furiously, but she didn't follow him up the stairs. With a swift hand she wiped the tears from her face. She went into the dark parlor and stayed there as I put my brothers and sister to bed.

A HARD, FEARFUL SLEEP overtook me. I kept seeing James Ackerman's kind, wise face, and I kept crying to him that I was sorry. Then I was taken to Hezekiel's punishment. My body twisted and writhed away from him. He came after me swinging shovels, boards, and the hoe. I jumped and dodged, hitting against everything in the way. It felt so real and made me hurt so much it was a relief to be awakened from it.

"Shh," Mother whispered so softly that I thought I was dreaming. "Get dressed."

I nodded and sank back into the warmth of sleep. This would be a good sleep. Hezekiel was gone. Mother was now by my side, watching over me.

"Get up *now,*" she whispered, and pinched my arm fiercely. "Get dressed and come downstairs."

Somehow I put on my clothes and found my way downstairs. In the kitchen Rachel cuddled sleepily against Mother's shoulder. Eli's hair was ruffled up like a wet cat's, and he was grouchy, snarling and hissing at everything. Adam behaved as if he had never gone to bed. Like a little water bug, he scooted back and forth across the kitchen floor while Eli watched him, uncomprehending.

"Stop that!" Mother told him angrily. "Be still! Sit over there. Be quiet!"

"Look out the front window," she murmured to me. "Don't let anyone see you."

Wondering why she would tell me such, I stumbled through the dark hallway. The front of my dress wasn't buttoned right, and I stopped to undo it and start all over again. Finally I had the holes and buttons lined up right and looked like I had some sense about me. Peeking through the window of the front parlor, I saw Hezekiel across the road on his front porch. He was sitting in a rocking chair under the glare of the single porch light. My heart boomed faster. The shotgun rested on his knee.

"Look out the back," Mother said calmly when I reported back to her. She made Rachel stand up. "Wake up, Rachel. Do you hear me?"

"Will he hurt us?" My hands were shaking as I tried to help Mother awaken the sleepy child.

"No." Mother was unafraid. "He wants us to *think* he will. He does only what everyone lets him get by with."

"But he shot at Mrs. Monroe."

Mother made an unsympathetic gesture. "*That* woman."

"He fired the gun. I was there." I *knew* Hezekiel would get us.

"He didn't hit her, did he? Now go check the backyard. We don't have much time."

"If you aren't afraid he will shoot us, why are we doing it this way?"

I didn't understand adults at all. It seemed so clear to me what could happen with Hezekiel and that shotgun.

Mother patted the side of my face and smiled reassuringly at my brothers and sister. "It's easier this way on our feelings. If we sneak away and don't get caught, we won't have to hear ugly things. Now go check the back window."

I eased to the storage room and looked through the window from a safe angle. Two men were sitting on their haunches by the old well in our backyard. One of them looked like Deacon Motes. The one holding the small lantern was Deacon Caroll. They were watching our back door. My stapler! I panicked, wanting to take it with me.

"They've been here all night," Mother said wearily when I told her about the men. "I am afraid there's only one way out."

We all followed her into the dining room. Mother quietly opened the window.

"Not one sound," she warned, shaking her finger at us. "Sarah Ruth, you drop out the window and stay by the wall. Are you listening to me?"

"What about Father?"

"You can stay with Father and be beaten and punished in the morning by Hezekiel, or you can go with me to Aunt Lila's."

I hoisted myself up and dropped out the window. My dress poofed as I jumped.

"Keep them against the wall," Mother said to me. She helped the boys drop one by one out the window. "If you make any noise," she warned them, "Hezekiel will get you."

The boys hugged against the wall for dear life.

Rachel's legs dangled over the windowsill and she wouldn't let go of Mother. I had to pull her downward, then cover up her mouth as she started to cry. Mother dropped heavily to the ground soon after.

"Walk slowly to that bush beside the start of the field," she whispered, and pointed straight across. "Wait for us there."

The bush seemed miles away, and I wondered how long before one of the men would shoot at me in the dark. Finally I reached the bush and crouched low, waiting for everyone to follow. The fear renewed itself each time someone I loved came toward me. *Don't let them get shot,* I prayed, even for Eli. Finally Mother sneaked across, Rachel clinging to her skirt.

With all of us holding hands, Mother led the way deftly through the fields, moving farther and farther away from danger. Distant stars were blurred over with huge clouds in the sky, foretelling of rain. Dark green crop leaves brushed against our arms, making us itch. At the end of the field, Mother carefully held up the bottom of a barbwire fence section so we could crawl through. When she let go, the wire bounced up and down noisily, but we were already too far from any of Hezekiel's men to be heard.

Three fields had to be crossed in the dark before we came out onto the highway. Although we seemed to be quite safely away, Mother wouldn't let us near the pavement. "Stay close to the ditch," she told us.

I knew this ditch quite well.

I wondered about my school treasures, hidden in the well cover. Mother said we'd return soon enough, but I didn't think so. Some other Mennonite child would find the stapler and the tape. I wiped away a tear. I hoped he or she would understand the enormous value of it all.

An old black-and-white bird dog started following us. Adam kept promising the dog we'd find it some food, but Mother kept shooing it away.

We were tired by the time we reached the old cemetery with the toppled graves. We sat down to rest. The sky was growing lighter. It was almost morning. Adam pointed to a white grave decoration that had blue plastic flowers, a red plastic phone, and the glittery message GOD IS CALLING YOU.

We didn't know what to think of an outside world that expected dead people to answer phones. There was only one phone near Heart Colony, and Hezekiel deemed it necessary and legal for the leader of the colony to use it. No one else could touch it, although we were allowed to watch him use it to order supplies.

Adam ran up and touched the grave decoration. Mother scolded him and said we should be on our way and touch nothing. When everyone's back was turned, I approached the phone bravely, but couldn't bring myself to touch it.

Soon we would be at the WELCOME TO SLAPEASY sign. I walked a little faster, then felt Eli spit on me. Before I could ask him why he would do such when we were all so worn-out, I felt the light, cold rain patting me gently on my shoulders and head. Then it began to pour, soaking us through. We huddled closely together and hurried past the SlapEasy sign. I noticed for the first time that some of the whirlybird wings were broken and the white rocks spelling the message were lined up crookedly. The most miserable, guilty feeling in the world shook over my body, and I sobbed wearily. Because of my fascination for spelling words, I had caused all of this.

"Hush," Mother said simply. "I would rather it be this rain falling upon us than what is at home."

12

FIVE DRIPPING MENNONITE scarecrows waited patiently for Aunt Lila to open the door. If she was surprised to see us, she didn't let on.

I liked Aunt Lila's tiny house. The walls in the first room were barely pink, and soft, creamy carpet covered the floor. We dried off our feet and tried not to step too heavily on the nice rug. A lumpy beige sofa sat in the middle of the room. When we sat down we sank through.

"Get up, you'll ruin her couch," Mother said.

"Let the children be." Aunt Lila waved for us to sit back down. "Nobody's ever sat there before. I'm glad to see it full, especially with family."

I could have stayed right there and slept, but Aunt Lila made us get up and change into dry clothes. Adam and Eli had to sleep in Lila's dresses, but I was too tired to tease them. Aunt Lila busily gathered up quilts and blankets to make pallets, and we lay down wearily on that fluffy, cushioned floor. I fell asleep wondering how Mother had known exactly where Aunt Lila's house was. "Mary Helen's big mouth" was all Mother would say.

We slept most of the day. The sun came through the tiny windows and warmed the rumpled clothing, blankets, and worn-out children stretched across the room. Adam snored loudly. His leg was flung across Eli's stomach. Rachel had scooted almost under the couch, her mouth wide-open as she mumbled and slept. A refrigerator door opened and shut in the small kitchen. Water splashed in a bathtub down the hall. Aunt Lila's careful footsteps moved about, coming through the front room, leaving again. I never opened my eyes fast enough to catch a glimpse of her. Mother slept on the sofa. Even the grinding and squealing of her teeth did not prevent my falling asleep again. I knew when morning came, and later I knew when it was afternoon. Still we continued to sleep.

That night we squeezed together around the supper table. Aunt Lila faced us with a smile, but she was worried. Tomato sandwiches and water, that's all she had to feed us. She kept apologizing until Mother assured her tomorrow we would look for work and provide food for as long as we stayed there.

Aunt Lila nodded in relief. She got up to check on our clothes, drying scattered across the room. Nobody spoke of Father, but I knew we were all thinking of him. I didn't believe we'd ever be a family with a father again. That night I put my pallet close to Rachel's and began to tell the children a story I made up about an old possum.

Eli was cranky about having to sleep in a dress again, but he quieted down when I got to the part where Old Possum discovers it is the tree, not him, hanging upside down. Like the possum, we slept uneasily that night but were unable to do anything about it.

I thought we'd be going to work in the morning, but instead we were left sitting on the shiny benches outside the principal's office at SlapEasy School. Even Rachel was going to a class. The ceilings of the hallways were as grandly magnificent as the day I had won the spelling bee. It came to me that what I had wished for had happened, but not the way I had planned it. Not with the blood of Mr. Ackerman on my hands and without Father in our lives.

Rachel and I wore our hair down. She looked much older with her hair down and was proud of the fact that in SlapEasy children who were six could go to school to attend something called kindergarten. Aunt Lila had shortened our dresses and cut Adam's and Eli's hair. Four pairs of white canvas shoes scuffled back and forth under the bench.

The office door opened and a familiar-looking man approached me, smiling.

"We're so proud to have the county spelling champ at our school." He patted me on the head. "And we think highly of your aunt Lila."

"What does he mean about 'spelling champ'?" Eli asked as we followed the principal down the hallway. I couldn't answer. I didn't want the principal to know the rest of my family had not celebrated my win.

"Your grandfather Franks was the smartest man I ever met," the principal said, smiling back at us. "He could take apart any kind of machine and put it back together in better shape than if it were brand-new. He used to come into town and fix things for our school, back when *my* father was the principal, and your grandfather was the colony leader. Your homeroom is in there, Sarah."

The principal opened a door with the number four painted in gold on the frosted-glass window. "Your brothers and sister will be going to the other building."

I hesitated. I didn't know if I wanted my wish to come true anymore. This school was so big. I didn't know anyone.

I was pushed into the room. All of the students stared up at me and frowned. They pointed at my clothes and whispered to each other. A few of them laughed out loud. I turned to run and find my brothers and sister, but the teacher held me firmly by the arm.

"I believe I know you!" she said, and guided me to a desk in the first row.

Obediently I sat down. She patted me on the back and then announced, "Class, this is the spelling whiz from Heart that I was telling you about. This girl can spell *anything,* except maybe *bicycle,* right, Sarah?"

I smiled uneasily, then realized that the attractive, dark-haired, dark-skinned teacher was Cassie's mother.

After a while the students stopped staring at me. I was handed an information card asking about my address, and then a few minutes later it was taken away from me. A loud bell rang and everyone jumped from the desks and ran out of the room.

I looked at Cassie's mother.

"End of homeroom," she explained. "I'll walk you to your first class." She motioned for me to come out into the hallway.

Students bumped into us as they hurried past. Cassie's mother kept reaching out, slowing students down, tapping them in warning.

"Why did you leave Heart?" she asked. "Is that a town, or what?"

Mother had told us not to say anything that would get back to Hezekiel or Father. I stared at the new tennis shoes that were rubbing blisters on every part of my feet, and said nothing. Sticking my hand into my dress pocket, I felt crumpled paper, slightly damp, and it puzzled me. What had I stuck in there?

Cassie's mother misunderstood my confusion.

"You don't know why you left?"

I nodded. She shook her head consolingly, then opened the next classroom door. I was introduced to the teacher, whom I recognized as the announcer with the chunky legs from the spelling bee. After I sat down in the back of the room, I discreetly pulled the mysterious wet paper out of my pocket

Hezekiel Whittenstone. Deposit only. SlapEasy Bank of Progress.

I nearly dropped it in fright. *I should throw that nasty paper away*, I thought. It doesn't matter anymore. That old world was gone, and I was in a strange new one that didn't seem like much more fun. I stuck the paper back into my pocket, lest someone find it and send it to Hezekiel. Then he would know I was at this school.

The rest of my morning was just as bad. The students chosen to guide me around the school always seemed to lose me.

It wasn't until lunch that I saw Cassie. Dressed in bright green pants and a matching green top, she escorted me through the food line, selecting everything for me and plopping it onto my tray.

The cafeteria lady asked for my money or a lunch form. I didn't understand, and she started fussing at me angrily. Everyone in the cafeteria line stopped talking and listened. Cassie jerked the tray from my hands and slammed it down in front of the woman. Grabbing two forks, she said loudly, "That's okay. We'll share *my* tray."

I followed her out of the cafeteria line.

"I hate her," Cassie said, leading me across the room to one of the long tables. "I call her the pit-bull cook."

Everywhere I walked people were pointing. I wondered if my legs looked normal in the shorter dress.

After I sat down I felt them watching, wondering how I would eat. Every crumb that fell from my mouth was spotted and talked about. The corn bread was the only thing I could digest. All the cafeteria food had a thin coat of waxy grease, and everything was in little white paper cups. Cassie ate as if it were a feast. "My mother never cooks," she said.

I thought about Adam, Eli, and Rachel and wondered if they were just as lost and miserable.

"How do you like school so far?" Cassie was licking the edge of her spoon.

"I don't think I do." I stared down at my tightly folded hands. Everything was so closed-in and noisy at the school. I longed for the quiet of the fresh, open fields.

Just then the boy with the glasses whom I'd beat out at the spelling bee came by our table.

"Physiognomy," he said, leaning over.

"What?" I wiped nervously at my face. He stared at me through his thick glasses.

"He wants you to spell it," Cassie whispered in my ear.

"Oh . . ." I tried to remember how he had pronounced it.

A tight smile twisted from one side of his mouth, then he nodded at me piteously and moved on.

"P-h-y—," I frantically called after him, and some of the kids looked up and giggled. I wanted out of that lunchroom.

The afternoon classes moved quickly. Mrs. Monroe

passed by me in the hallway, stared in surprise, then came back to hug me.

"What are you doing here?" I asked her.

"A teacher left on maternity leave, so I am taking her place until she returns sometime around the end of November." Mrs. Monroe smiled. "What are *you* doing here? Helping them with their spelling?"

"No." I sighed. "I'm only making people mad with my spelling."

"I miss having my own little school and being free to spend more individual time with my students," Mrs. Monroe said, tousling my hair. "I miss my favorite student."

If there had been more time before the tardy bell, we would have talked ourselves into a good cry, but we had to turn loose and go to separate classrooms. So Mrs. Monroe wasn't very happy here, either. *It all could have been so different,* I thought, not caring how evil this sounded, *if Hezekiel had not jumped away from Mrs. Monroe's car.*

The boy with glasses passed by me in the hallway.

"Persnickety," he said.

"Rude," I answered. "R-u-d-e."

WHEN THE BELL RANG at the end of the day, Aunt Lila was waiting for us by the elementary playground.

"It was fun, wasn't it?" she asked excitedly. Her thin face was flushed. I knew she was thinking of her own children and wanting this for them as well.

"We're not supposed to have fun," Eli said. "I didn't like the other school, and now I'm in one that's got more of everything I didn't like."

"*I* like it," I said, only for Aunt Lila's sake. She smiled, pleased.

"Where's Mother?" Adam asked.

"She got the janitorial job at the bank," Aunt Lila said, smiling. "She'll be home soon."

"A teacher said I can't breathe good because of my *Gs*," Rachel said unhappily.

"She was the school nurse, a nurse practitioner, like a doctor," Aunt Lila explained. "I told her about your allergies, Rachel. She said she could help. She thinks you have asthma, and she'll fix you up so you'll be able to breathe better. She's the one who found the house for me to stay in."

"What's she gonna do to me?" Rachel asked suspiciously. "I don't like school, not if it's gonna be about breathing."

A huge truck carrying shiny new cars stacked on top of one another zoomed by, blowing my hair into my face.

"*Whoooooeeeeeee!*" Adam jumped up and down. "Let's go get us a car!"

I caught him by the shoulder as he tried to chase the truck. "No! We can't get those."

Convinced I was wrong, he gave me an exaggerated, hurt expression. "Then where does everybody get their cars?"

"They buy them," Aunt Lila said, shouting over the noise of the traffic.

"The town buys them? They don't share?"

"No. This isn't like the colony. Everybody here owns things by themselves."

Adam blinked at me in disbelief, then shook his head, unconvinced. The way he watched that truck drive away worried me.

"Try to not get so excited over everything," I said to all of them. "People won't understand it's all so new to us. They'll think we're just simple-minded."

At Aunt Lila's house Mother was already back from her new job. Right away she noticed the shorter dresses and the boys' haircuts.

"Lila, what have you done to my children?"

"You want to stay here. You have to fit in."

"But we're not staying here. As soon as Solomon comes to his true feelings, we will be going with him to Cousin Amelia's."

"But are you not curious about life in the outside world?" Aunt Lila asked.

"I'm more concerned with how I will live in the afterlife. I plan on being rewarded for my faith and my show of modesty. Live simple and plain, clean of sin, for this time on earth is short compared to what follows."

"I think God is more concerned with our deeds than our clothes, Hannah."

"You still dress like a Mennonite."

"Yes, but I'm not a child that gets stared at in school."

"I didn't want them in that school."

"It's the law, and if we live here, we have to abide by it."

"I want the children the way they looked yesterday." Mother's crossed arms meant serious trouble.

"The boys' hair will grow back," Aunt Lila said. "But what I cut off the girls' skirts, I threw away."

13

A LOW MURMUR of voices awakened me. Scooting forward on my elbows, I managed to peer around the corner of the sofa. The kitchen was lit up cheerfully while the dark gloom of morning pressed against the windows. Mother and Aunt Lila were examining a crumpled wad of paper. Two very sinful, steaming cups of coffee were in front of them on the table.

"I found it in the pocket before washing her dress last night."

"It's what I needed! All I have to do is give them this number at the top and ask for an account-history printout of how much was put in the bank and when."

"What if they say no?"

"They won't. I had them run a history of my account, and all I gave them was the number. I'm not worried." Aunt Lila sipped her coffee.

"You might not be worried, but I am. What if the bank people see it is Hezekiel's account that you want?"

"I'm still legally married to him, aren't I? As his wife I have a right to see those papers on the bank account, although he thinks I have no rights because I married him."

"Remember when I married Solomon?" Mother giggled and stared up at the kitchen cabinets as if they, too, were listening. "He was so nervous, he couldn't repeat the words right."

Lila nodded. "Hezekiel added words that were not supposed to be said at our wedding. He added rules on what a wife couldn't do and the things a husband could do."

"Why did you marry him?"

"I thought he loved me. There weren't many choices unless I wanted to marry our cousin David and have babies dying young of cousins' disease."

"I loved Solomon." Mother sighed. "He smiled so easy at me, all the time, and not at anybody else that way. I made him happy without trying."

"I never made Hezekiel happy."

"Nor he you," Mother reminded her. "Solomon isn't quick to anger like Hezekiel. He thinks everything through first."

"I know you still love him, but I don't love Hezekiel and never did. He's done wrong things. You and I both did the right thing by leaving them and the colony."

"I don't know." Mother sipped at the coffee. "Lila, did you have an interest in the truck driver who brought supplies to the colony?"

"Oh, yes," Lila said happily. "He always smiled at me, but I only sinned in my mind. Nothing ever happened."

"That's good." Mother took another sip of her coffee.

"After I left the colony, I called him. I knew his work number from the delivery receipts at the colony. Nothing ever happened because *he* wasn't interested. Being friendly was just his way of greeting everybody, not just me. Now, how about going in the bank with me to get those papers?"

"No. I don't want to lose my job there."

"We won't get in trouble. The worst thing they could do is say no. But with you beside me, they'll probably say yes. I can go in early with you to clean before it opens."

AUNT LILA MUST have convinced Mother, because the next morning as Mother walked us to school, she told us Aunt Lila was going to help clean up the bank, but I knew what she *really* meant. I thought I deserved some praise for finding that important bit of paper, but I kept my compliments to myself. Aunt Lila had already gone ahead of us because Adam and Eli walked too slow, she said, and she needed to get a cup of coffee at the BetterBagging deli. Adam and Eli trudged just behind me and Rachel, and wore the most mournful looks about going to school that I'd ever seen in my entire life. It was much more mournful than the way they looked the first day of our going to public school, and that had been pretty sad.

I noticed the crude vegetable stand first and nudged my mother to look. Chicken wire nailed to the sides of the little lean-to protected it from the outside world. Heavy black plastic draped over the top formed a saggy roof, which was held down with loose boards. A long wooden counter was propped across two barrels. In front of the counter, dark red tomatoes, yellow squash, and green bell peppers were all displayed in big wooden baskets.

"It's Naomi!" Mother said excitedly. "Wait here."

She crossed the street, dodging cars recklessly. She was going to ask about Father, I knew from the hopeful smile on her face. Naomi and the other two women saw her coming and turned their backs. Mother hesitated, then made up her mind to go over to them, anyway.

She bent over and picked out a green bell pepper from the basket. I could see her asking the price. Still the women refused to turn around. Mother dug into her dress pocket for a coin. She set it on the counter and stepped back, waiting for them to take it.

Naomi glanced sideways, then said something to the other women. Mother shook her head no. Cautiously she reached to touch Naomi's arm. Naomi leaped back, knocking the other two women against the chicken wire. Leaning across the counter, Mother pleaded with them, but they moved to the back of the makeshift building and covered their ears.

Gesturing hopelessly, Mother left them and returned toward us. Staring at the green pepper in her hand, she tried not to cry. Suddenly Naomi came out from the shed and ran after her.

"He's suffering because of *you*! You should see what you've caused for your husband!"

Mother was so startled she stopped in the middle of the street and dropped the bell pepper. She let it lie there and ran to us as if *we* were in danger.

"Don't listen. Please don't listen." She grabbed for our hands. "Let's go."

Naomi bent down and picked up the pepper from the street. She carried it back to the vegetable stand and dropped it into the basket.

Mother kept hurrying us along.

"I want to see Father!" Rachel screamed over and over all the way to school. By the time we got there, my ears were worn-out. I left Rachel, Mother, Adam, and Eli and climbed the big steps of my building for more torture. My face broke out in red blotches. I felt very guilty. I had caused all of this.

In the classroom everyone stared and pointed at my dress like they had the day before. By the end of the day, though, I had solved that problem forever.

Unfortunately it wasn't Aunt Lila waiting for us after school. Mother took one look at my short, pink-flowered dress and refused to walk with me.

"I can't change back into my Mennonite dress." I trailed foolishly behind my family.

"Yes, you can. Get away from us."

"Cassie traded my dress for hers. She's wearing it, and I don't know where she lives."

Mother eyed me suspiciously. "Why would she want a Mennonite dress? It isn't her religion."

I turned red. Cassie *had* given me her dress, but she wore her gym clothes home. My Mennonite dress was in a trash can at school, wrapped in newspaper so Aunt Lila wouldn't see it while cleaning the rest room.

"Everyone makes fun of me because I wear the same dress every day."

"Well, it's *clean* every day," Mother said angrily over her shoulder. "When we get to Aunt Lila's, we're going to fit one of her dresses on you."

God was still punishing me for that spelling bee. Aunt Lila's dresses were big and ugly. How could I ever go back to school? But maybe this is what I deserved for causing James Ackerman to die while waiting for the car.

I trudged behind Mother and tried to keep myself free from the sinful urge to scream and stomp around. We passed the empty corner where earlier the vegetable stand had been. I wished the women had stayed so my new dress would send them into a high-spun fit.

At the house Mother searched for Aunt Lila's Mennonite dresses to no avail. Guessing that Aunt Lila was washing the dresses at a Laundromat, Mother sat down on the sofa beside me and waited. I scooted over to the deepest edge. *Just let her try and take this dress off me,* I thought. I loved the pink flowers and the soft way the fabric flowed across my skin. I was wearing this dress to school tomorrow.

The door opened then, and a SlapEasy woman stepped into Aunt Lila's house. We all stared up at her. She had on purple pants and a silky purple-and-white shirt. Her bright blond hair was short and curly, her eyes blue and happy.

Aunt Lila?

"From now on I am a different person."

Mother looked at her suspiciously.

"It's my own money, Hannah," Aunt Lila said. "The school gave me a paycheck today."

She handed out blue jeans and green plaid shirts for the boys, a red ruffled dress with a big red bow for Rachel, and nothing for me.

"You *have* your new dress," Aunt Lila said matter-of-factly. "I saw you leaving the school rest room with it on, so I bought something for your mother instead."

"No, no. None of us can wear these—"

"Don't be so harsh, Hannah." Aunt Lila dug into the large bag. "You've *left* the colony."

She held up the most beautiful, short dress I've ever seen.

Mother gasped softly, then the hard look came back over her.

"Put it away. I'm not going to change from what I am."

"You don't have to change what is inside you." Aunt Lila dropped the dress into Mother's lap.

"Inside is outside. That is why we live as we do."

"They say Hezekiel is a man of God, because of what is on his outside."

"What is inside me," Mother said, flustered and angry, "is of God, not the same as Hezekiel."

"Then clothes make no difference." Aunt Lila crunched up the paper sack and threw it across the room. "Wear the dress. I know you like it. Besides, it almost looks like a Mennonite dress, except for the length and the color."

"What color do you call this?" Mother touched the delicate sleeves and the tiny round buttons. "It isn't quite pink."

"Peach. It would be pretty on you."

Mother blushed guiltily. She kept staring at the dress and touching it, then tried to look away and couldn't.

Slowly she reached her decision. "I will pay you next Friday for the dress, after I've bought something for the children, and paid for our food and lodging with you."

"I know the bank doesn't pay much for janitorial services," Aunt Lila said with a laugh. "Just pay me whenever you can. It doesn't have to be next Friday."

THE FAMILY PASSING through the huge mirrored doors of the Pizza House that evening was not us. The vivid colors, the laughter, that had to belong to SlapEasy people. Or that's what the people of SlapEasy thought. For the first time ever, we were not stared at. We went through the salad bar, made numerous trips to the buffet table, and not once did people point or whisper.

I didn't care too much for pizza, but my brother Eli, for the first time since leaving the colony, found something about SlapEasy he loved. He stacked, seasoned, forked, and shoved all the pizza within his new-shirted reach. Every time he breathed out, I smelled peppercorns and pizza.

I couldn't bear much more and was grateful when Rachel wanted me to take her to the rest room. I hoped that when I returned Eli would have been given a table of his own to spread out and burp in.

The rest rooms were beside a huge room with machines that beeped and flickered flashes of light. Mother had told us not to look in there, so I hurried past, my head high, Rachel clutching my hand.

"Sarah Ruth!"

The low voice of the dead! Shivering, I made myself turn toward that bad room and the wondrous ghost face of my one true love.

A very alive Joshua Mueller stood there grinning. His hair was short and his clothes were very outside world. The only thing he still wore of the colony was the deep scar on his forehead.

"Your parents have been searching the creek for you!" My mouth hung open, and my heart was going *thumpity-thump.*

He shrugged. "I left my clothes in the water."

"They've searched night after night for you. They think you're dead! Don't you care?"

He squinted angrily, and the scar over his forehead puckered. "They didn't care about me. They were going to let him hurt me. He would have killed me."

"They wouldn't have let him touch you. Didn't you hear your mother pleading for mercy and your father saying he would punish you and Hezekiel didn't need to?"

"I heard everybody thinking I was guilty and Hezekiel picking up that shovel."

"Your father would have stopped him. My father would have stopped him."

"Like they did last time? When he did *this* to me?" Joshua pointed to the scar. "Everybody cared more for the new boy, who really was a sinner, than they did me. So now they got him and I took his place out here. Fair and even trade."

"Not for your parents. They no longer have a son."

"They got the church. My family does everything they're told to do in church."

"They don't go to church anymore, not since you left. They've been defying Hezekiel."

He shrugged slightly, then smiled. "I knew *you'd* be in SlapEasy one day. I saw your picture in the paper. Did they kick you out?"

I shook my head. "No. We left."

"All but your father."

"How did you know that?"

"He's not in there with the rest of your family. Didn't you see me earlier? I sat two tables away from you."

He had grown so much older, I thought, and so changed. Something unexplainable kept me guarding my smile and my words. Perhaps it was the dark emotion in his eyes. Or the realization that I still found him more exciting than all the temptations of Slap-Easy.

He sensed my fear and moved away from me to the mirrored doors leading outside.

"You know James Ackerman died," I said carefully.

"Yeah. My boss told me Hezekiel made the ambulance bring Deacon Ackerman into town even though he was dead when they got there. The ambulance driver said he died instantly when the tractor turned over, you could tell by looking down at his neck. But Hezekiel insisted on going in the ambulance with him and pretending he might make it. He said everybody who was there had to know the man was dead, but they kept listening to Hezekiel."

I was stunned. Our not being there with the car had nothing to do with the death! But others besides Hezekiel must have known it. Why didn't anyone tell Father? Was *everyone* at Heart Colony so against us they were willing to tell lies along with Hezekiel?

"Do you think I set the fire?" Joshua asked.

"No. I know you didn't."

He searched my face for a sign of deception, then decided I was being honest.

"Are you glad you left?"

"No," I said truthfully.

"You can't go back. They'll never let you. You always

wanted to be in the outside world. You know you did."

"It isn't as beautiful as it seemed in the schoolbooks."

"So? Heart Colony isn't beautiful, either."

"It used to be." My eyes watered. "If my father had become the new leader, it would be more beautiful there than it is here."

"That will never happen. Do you know what Hezekiel did to me? He told me to get a shovel from the Schumpert shed. I went in and he bolted the door behind me. I couldn't get out. Then he must have set fire to the house. I thought I was going to die as the fire moved closer. I thought of you, and how I'd never see you again."

I blushed and looked down at Rachel. She was twisting my fingers violently, and I had to shake back my hand.

"I got to use the bathroom," she said.

"Please tell your parents that you're here." I tried to look sincere, but Rachel was pulling me down the hall.

"I don't want Hezekiel to know where I am." He handed me a small picture and took off. "Give them this."

I looked down at the picture. Joshua was standing in front of an orange building and his hair was still in the Mennonite cut. I treasured this even more than the school stapler, even though I knew I would have to do the right thing and send it on.

14

THE WRETCHED GROANS echoed down the hallway from the bathroom. Because of Eli I couldn't hear Mother and Aunt Lila talking in the kitchen. The long white papers in their hands contained Hezekiel's banking history. I heard Aunt Lila say, "I'll copy them tomor—," before Eli drowned her out again.

I snuggled into the sofa and smiled. Joshua was alive and had seen me just hours before in this pretty dress with the pink flowers. I patted the deep hem of the skirt. Joshua's picture was tucked safely inside. No one had noticed when I took a needle and thread to the privacy of Aunt Lila's room to rip out a section of hem and loosely hand sew it back, and no one knew I had seen Joshua. Rachel had given me some trouble on the walk from the Pizza House, asking me about the strange boy from SlapEasy. In her confusion over so much new, she hadn't listened to what we were saying. Her attention had been given instead to all those beeps and flashing lights of the game room. Soon I would have to tell Mother and Aunt Lila all the important details Joshua had told me, but then I'd have to relinquish the photo. I wanted to enjoy it and this secret love just a little bit longer. I would also have to make sure nobody washed my dress with the photo in it.

"*Sarah,* I'm talking to you." Aunt Lila tapped me on the shoulder. "I'm going to the store to get Eli some medicine. Do you want to go?"

"No," I said dreamily.

I recalled Joshua's confession and blushed. He had thought about me while almost dying in that fire. Perhaps that was why he was spared from the fire—for me. Where would we live? Would we wear Mennonite clothing? What about our children?

"What's worrying you?" Mother came into the room and switched on the lights.

"The Pizza House." I sighed.

"If you're going to throw up, go into the kitchen. Don't stay here on the carpet."

"I'm not going to throw up. I'm not a hog like Eli," I said, but Mother had gone back down the hall to the bathroom.

Piercing sirens and red flashing lights invaded the house, then passed on to disturb the other houses. I ignored the insignificance of it all until the front door banged open and Aunt Lila tore past me.

"Oh, it's a bad thing! Come look!" she cried.

Everyone but Eli followed her outside. The flashing red lights went around the corner and four blocks up. We followed quickly along the sidewalk. People came out of their houses and joined our curious group. More police cars and fire trucks whizzed by, knocking my breath off beat each time a siren sneaked up behind. Around the fourth corner we could see to the end of Main Street. Lights flashed in front of the stately, columned antebellum courthouse. Even though the judicial white walls were not ablaze, the fire trucks surrounded the well-manicured lawn. We hurried on for another block, until we could see a red truck cab turned over, a long silvery tank torn from it and on its side across the courthouse lawn. The strong odor of gasoline traveled heavily in our direction.

"What happened?" Aunt Lila stopped a fireman to ask. He had the nicest smile and spent all of it on Aunt Lila.

"Gas spill, Lila. One of those darned county prisoners escaped from jail over there and jumped right into this truck as it stopped for the red light up yonder. The driver scared so badly, he fell out. His foot went off the brake, the truck rolled downhill to the courthouse and tipped over. We're evacuating this area 'cause hundreds of gallons of gas keep pouring out. See it over there?"

"Why do we have to leave?" Aunt Lila fluffed up the back of her new hair.

"One spark and *kabooooom!* There goes our courthouse!

"Don't worry," he added, seeing the panic on her face, "the Mennonites are coming to help."

That's all it took for Aunt Lila. She was gone.

The fireman looked disappointed. "The Mennonites don't mind doing hard labor for free when there's an emergency," he said to us, but without Aunt Lila's presence he didn't seem as friendly. "It could take several days for a professional cleanup team to get here, and we don't have the time to wait." He glanced around one more time in the direction Aunt Lila had taken, then walked back to join the other firemen. Our panic now intensified, Mother moved us further down the street, almost to the corner.

"Go with Aunt Lila." She nudged Rachel, Adam, and me in the direction of the house. Rachel and Adam obediently left. I remained right where I was.

"Are you staying?" I asked Mother. I hoped not.

"If I can just see him and know he's in good health."

"Hezekiel might see us!"

"Us?" she hesitated, then sighed. "We'll wait over here, where he can't see us."

"Father might not come with the others."

"Your father always helps when there is a need. He's a good man."

White halos from the streetlights lit the sidewalk. Mother and I moved into the darker shadows. Up ahead, the firemen set up roadblocks and caution markers. Reflections of red and blue lights chased around the walls of the courthouse. The ground grew mushy, filling with fuel. The boots of the firemen sank as they walked along the edges of the lawn. The gas was now fully soaking into the ground, and there no longer was such a direct danger of fire, but a bigger environmental danger. The tanker would have to be moved and the gas-soaked dirt removed. The fire hose was extended and the firemen sprayed a soft, foamy substance that was quickly absorbed into the ground.

A truck with a yellow flashing light and a huge rusty hook on the back pulled up beside the fire trucks. The driver extended long chains and thick black belts to the overturned tank. He moved quickly, wrapping the tank and securing it. The firemen lined up on one side to help. The chains tightened and squealed. There was a heavy crunching noise and then the tank lifted slightly off the ground. With the help of the firemen, the tank was righted. I covered my nose. Even three blocks away the fumes ruled the air.

The men shouted orders at each other as another truck with yellow lights arrived, one with a long, flat bed. Then the tank was hoisted onto the flatbed truck, only I could not see how because the fire truck was in the way. Both yellow-light trucks drove away, with the tank on one and the wrecked cab dragging from the big hook on the other.

Everyone then settled into an uneasy waiting and watching. The firemen sat and talked, guarding the still potentially explosive area. The red lights were shut off on the fire trucks. The blue lights on the police cars remained flashing. Mother stood up and stretched. Purple twilight changed into black night as my mother continued to worry me.

I watched the streets until my eyes ached for new scenery.

"Maybe the fireman was wrong. They aren't coming."

"He wasn't mistaken."

And then I heard it—the loud grumbling of Heart's backhoe. It came puttering and gliding around the corner, followed by the water truck and the dull brown station wagon.

"He's here!" Mother said, her hand shaking as she tried to cover her mouth.

As she stared at the brown mud dauber, I wondered if I should tell Mother the ambulance story that Joshua had told me. She needed to know it wasn't our fault. But then she would want to know whom I had heard it from and I'd have to tell her everything. If I told anything at all about seeing Joshua, she might not let me see him again, even if she was convinced he'd had nothing to do with the fire. He was an "outsider" now, and we weren't to make ourselves too familiar with any of them. I stared at the car, looking for Father.

Mr. Schumpert drove the backhoe. The men from the colony jumped out of the station wagon and the colony water truck. They carried shovels and nodded silently to the firemen. They passed fearlessly through the warning circle of trucks and stepped out into the disaster area. The pants legs of their overalls were rolled up. Barefoot, they stood in the contaminated soil and began digging up layer upon layer. The soggy mounds of dirt were shoveled onto the back of the farm truck, which no longer had the water tank on it.

Mother watched Father's steady moves. "I'm so proud of him." Her eyes brimmed with tears.

I nodded, ready to go. This could only end badly. I could feel it.

"You see how hard he's working? We do good things for the outsiders. Not everyone talks about it, but we do. During the flood five years ago, the Mennonites cleaned up the stale water."

Yes, I nodded. *Oh, please, let's go, before they see us.*

"When my father was the leader, we always did nice things for others, like the Mennonites at Cousin Amelia's colony do. Their firemen work with the city, help with their fires, it's allowed. You can have jobs outside the colony."

There was no stopping her. She was working up her convictions and working on my last nerve. She started to pace. Soon she was worrying out loud.

"What if someone throws a match out there? What if one of the outsiders forgets?"

"They won't. It would blow *all* of us up."

That didn't affect her as I'd hoped it would. She remained right where she was.

The men kept shoveling. The back of the farm truck sagged from the heavy load of greasy dirt. Hezekiel jumped into the truck and drove off.

Mother took off, too.

She ran down the street, to a new disaster.

"Solomon!"

Father put down his shovel.

"Solomon. Come here." She gestured friendly

enough. She stood on the edge of the gas-soaked lawn.

"Why are you here?" he shouted.

Every fireman and Mennonite stopped working and looked up. The red lights flashed again from the tops of the fire trucks.

"I want you to be careful."

He ignored her and kept digging.

She tried again. "Please, look at me, Solomon."

He did. Father stared at her loosened hair bun and the short peach dress. "I do not know you, dressed like that."

Mother shook her head, not accepting his answer, and began to babble nervously. "Soon you will be leader. We have the proof against Hezekiel. I miss you, and your children miss you. So very much."

The Mennonite men started talking loudly, angrily, to each other and to Father, then pointed at Mother. We were in trouble. Mother knew that, yet she started stepping onto the dangerous soil toward him.

Father's face convulsed. The terrible headache was pushing through him fast. "Be gone, sinful woman!"

He threw the shovel in her direction. It landed with a sharp clink on the pavement, too far away to have harmed her. She turned and ran like a young girl.

Rage and love and fear twisted inside me. The colony had taken all of us and wrung the family out, leaving knotted-up hearts bumping this way and that, trying to untangle themselves.

I caught my mother and put my arms around her, and told her not to cry. The colony men were all watching us as we braved our way under the harsh lights and around the corner.

"He loves his children. He didn't mean that." Mother leaned her head into my shoulder. "Don't let it upset you. You know he loves you."

It wasn't the children he had directed his anger at, I wanted to argue, for the sake of truth. But Mother knew that and began to cry as the truth forced its way through her. I wouldn't cry. He wasn't my father anymore, not as long as he behaved like Hezekiel. I glanced worriedly behind me. I had a fear we were being followed.

"I'm taking this dress back to the store." Mother was no longer crying.

"But why?" I argued. "It's such a beautiful dress."

"Not if it causes me to lose your father."

"Don't *you* like the dress?"

"Of course I do, but I can't wear it anymore." She flung open the front door to Aunt Lila's, and we faced the wildest mess of a front room. Pillows, clothing, and unopened cans of coffee were piled in the middle of the floor. Rachel and Adam ran back and forth dropping soap, towels, and toothpaste into the pile. Eli, still sick from the pizza, had moved from the bathroom to the kitchen sink. Aunt Lila was shrieking through the house, "I've got to get away. He's gonna get me!"

"Stop this!" With one precise movement of her arm, Mother set Adam and Rachel on the couch. Plastic bottles spilled out of their hands.

"Make them stay here." She left me in charge of the children sitting on the couch.

She hurried to the kitchen to assess Eli's condition, and decided to leave him standing there at the sink.

"Lila, stop this. Stop it right now!" I heard her say as she entered the tiny bedroom. "Lila, Lila."

"He's going to hit me. He saw me. I know he did. He'll find my house. He'll beat me. My hair was finally starting to grow out, and he'll snatch it from my scalp again."

"Not if you don't let him. Remember, you are a different person now, inside and outside. Look at how you've survived moving away from there. You have a house and food, and you've been so good to us. You've taken care of us. You're a strong person now, Lila."

"That won't stop him from hurting me." Aunt Lila was a little calmer; at least she wasn't screaming her words.

"He can't touch you outside the colony. You're safe here. There are all those firemen to make him stop. Think about the children. You're scaring them. Let the firemen take care of this."

There was a long pause, and then Aunt Lila said, "Hannah, the firemen put out the fires and the police keep people away."

"I know that, but I thought you liked that fireman. And how do you expect Hezekiel to find you and recognize you without your gray bun?"

Unexpectedly, Aunt Lila laughed. The scare was over. We weren't going anywhere. This warm, cozy house with the soft carpet and pink walls was still my home. And somewhere in this town, maybe only a few streets away, Joshua sat thinking about me and how pretty I looked in this pink-flowered dress. I hung up my dress and got ready for bed.

I WAS RIDING in the old farm truck. The floorboard rattled and jolted my feet. There was nowhere to put them. The truck was falling apart. I fell with it, with every bump, then woke up.

Stretched out on a pallet, I realized I wasn't in the farm truck, but the floor was still shaking. Tremors shook through my entire body, jittering the furniture lightly and bouncing me above the thick padding of carpet.

An earthquake! Mrs. Monroe had showed me pictures once. The ground was going to crack open, splitting apart the house and all the wool twigs of the carpet. We'd slide downward, into the unknown.

"Get up!" I screamed, tugging at my mother's shoulder. "It's an earthquake!"

Mother mumbled something and kept her eyes closed. "Sleep."

I tried to roll her off the couch. "You can't sleep. We'll all die!"

Eli, Adam, and Rachel popped up from the pallets.

"Is she sick?" Adam asked, referring to me.

"The floor is shaking." I couldn't tell them of the horrors waiting below.

Mother put her hand down. Then she sat up to feel the sides of the couch. "Something *is* shaking . . ."

"It's an earthquake, and we have to move— I don't remember where!" So much responsibility rested on me in this catastrophe. I was the A student and the spelling champ. I was supposed to know these things. I could spell it. E-A-R-T—

"Quick! Everybody get in a doorway!" Adam shouted. *How did he know what to do?* I wondered. He had hardly gone to school. But it sounded right.

I was racing toward the front door, but my clothing was not. Mother held firmly to the skirt of the big sleeping dress.

"Hush!" she said.

A soft moaning reminded me of Eli sick in the bathroom, but Eli was right beside me. Tiny worry lines spread across Mother's face.

Aunt Lila entered the room, clutching the sides of her loose nightdress. "He's come after me."

She moaned again, frightened. The worry lines vanished from Mother's face.

"Oh, Lila," she said. "I thought a child was sick. Calm down. Nobody is going to get you."

Aunt Lila said nothing. She kept staring toward the heavy beige curtains of the front window.

Mother tiptoed to the front window and peered out. The floor shook harder and the doorknob rattled. Rachel started crying. Mother hurried back over.

"They're trying to scare us. Lie back down and pretend not to hear." She held Rachel close. "It won't last long. The police will drive by and see it and make them leave."

Aunt Lila sank to her knees and clenched her hands together in prayer.

"What are they doing?" I asked.

"Stomping their feet. Hezekiel calls it stamping. It hasn't been done in a long time. They won't harm us. They're just loudly showing us their disapproval. Hezekiel has them all surrounding the house, all except your father. I know he's not out there." Mother sounded a little doubtful.

I huddled next to her. Foot stomping closed in around us. The muffled thundering shook the windows, then rippled around the sides of the house. First by the front door, then the deafening sound on the tiny wooden back porch. I didn't understand why they would do such. I wanted them to stop.

"It won't last long. The neighbors will hear it," Mother kept reassuring us. "Tomorrow, Lila, we need to see about getting a telephone."

Aunt Lila nodded absently, her lips still moving in prayer. Eli and Adam took turns pressing their hands against the smooth hall floor to feel the vibrations. For all her brave words, Mother was shaking.

"They don't do these kinds of things in other Mennonite colonies," Mother said. "In other colonies you can leave and folks leave you alone."

"I think I see Daniel out there," Aunt Lila said happily as she peered through the front window.

"If it is him he's doing something bad," Mother cautioned her. "He's stomping us."

"Yes, but at least I know both precious feet are alive and still moving." Aunt Lila moved away from the window.

I hurried into the hallway and snatched up my new pink-flowered dress. Then I saw the small folded pad of Hezekiel's bank slips on the counter and slipped them into the dress hem by Joshua's picture. If Hezekiel got into the house, at least he would not get these.

The noise grew even louder around us.

"I'm sorry I brought this upon us," Aunt Lila said. "But if I had stayed, if I had not come here, I would be dead by now."

"I don't think he would have killed you." Mother tried so hard to smile at Lila. "I know he hurt you, though."

I tried not to look at Aunt Lila and cause her greater grief, but I knew what her eyes were remembering. When she thought all of us were asleep earlier, I had heard her confess her shame to Mother that she had let Hezekiel hit her over and over again without moving, just standing there.

"No." Aunt Lila turned away so we could see only the small lift to her shoulders every time she breathed. "By my own hands, not Hezekiel's, I would be... gone."

"Then you should face up to him and let *him* be afraid of *you*. That is the only cure."

Quiet came all at once. Had it been hours or only minutes? The thunder echoed only in our thoughts now as we listened hard. The night was silent and empty.

"I'm going to see."

Before Mother could get the chains and bolt undone, Aunt Lila threw herself against the door.

"Don't! They want us to come out so they can get us."

Mother gently moved her out of the way. "I'm not afraid of them. They need to know it. Then they'll leave us alone."

She opened the door and shouted, "God sees you in your shame! Shame on you for coming here to scare two helpless women and four small children."

Aunt Lila hesitated, then she stepped outside, her short blond curls gleaming under the porch light.

"I am a new woman!" she called out. "Hezekiel Whittenstone, I am not afraid of you!"

"That was good." Mother patted her on the shoulder. They stepped inside and shut and bolted the door.

Blam! The door was struck by a hard object from the other side. Aunt Lila jumped straight up into the air. Then, surprisingly, she snatched up some plates and in a fury opened the door and threw them with all of her might. The plates shattered in the street, breaking the uneasy silence. Aunt Lila put her hand on her hip and waited. No other sounds followed.

"Did you see that nice fireman I was talking to at the

courthouse tonight?" Aunt Lila still looked angry but fluffed up her hair with her fingers. "His name is Tim. We usually drink coffee together in the morning at the BetterBagging deli. He seems so nice. I wonder what it's like to have a husband that isn't mean?"

15

SOME BOY WAS READING to the class when the principal knocked on the door and handed our teacher a note. Half asleep from the night's turmoil, I didn't hear what the teacher then said to the class.

My hand touched the hem of my pink-flowered dress, confirming Joshua's picture had not forsaken me. Mother, so good at searching my dress pockets, would certainly inspect a suspicious hemline, especially when I had refused to let her wash the dress. She was already angry about that, and finding a picture of an "outsider" boy would certainly make her angrier. Then there would be the lecture about finding a proper husband at Cousin Amelia's colony, like I'd heard last night. Rachel had apparently told on me for talking to a boy at the Pizza House. I had been warned once again this morning not to speak to SlapEasy boys and not to go in the school rest room before Aunt Lila had cleaned it. I would have to give the photo up today and tell Aunt Lila and Mother what they needed to know about Hezekiel and the fire.

"Sarah Ruth." The chunky-legged teacher didn't need a microphone like she had at the spelling bee. My name roared across the room so that everyone in the entire building was aware of my transgression. "I said, put up your reading builder workbook and get out a pen or pencil plus one sheet of clean notebook paper."

Several students giggled, but then, they had been making fun of me all morning for wearing the same dress to school two days in a row. At lunch they'd made fun of me for talking like I was "from the olden days," and I left the cafeteria when the boy in glasses sauntered in, his *Webster's Dictionary* strapped onto his lunch box. And now here I was in the worst class of the day with the chunky-legged teacher.

"Sarah Ruth," she shouted. "One clean sheet of paper! Now!"

"Oh." I shoved the reading workbook under my desk and grabbed my spiral notebook. I hesitated. I hated tearing pages out of my notebook. If I kept that up, soon they would all be gone, and paper was so expensive. Mother said one notebook each was all we could ever get.

The other students were ripping pages out of their notebooks and then carelessly ripping them up before finally settling on one perfect sheet.

"Today we are writing a thank-you to the Heart

Colony Mennonites for all their hard work last night."

Astonished, I looked up at my teacher. *Thank* them for stomping around the house and saying hurtful things to Mother? *Thank* them for keeping us awake and frightened most of the night? Not me. I crumpled that paper up and threw it to the ground.

"I said everyone." The teacher was staring right at me.

I stared back.

"Sarah Ruth Heart. Paper and pen. Do you need to borrow some?"

The student behind me snickered. I guessed they'd never forget how I came to school with no supplies the first day.

"No, ma'am."

"Then start writing."

"No, ma'am," I said in a whisper.

The teacher walked over to my desk. "In *this* school, everyone has to do what the teacher says. Why are you refusing to do this?"

Why didn't she understand that if I told her everything, I'd be bringing the wrath of Hezekiel upon my family and this school?

"You can't sit there and refuse to do it without a reason."

"My reason is—I don't want to."

Most of the class laughed. The teacher snapped her fingers angrily at me. "You want to clown? *You* go to the principal's office. *Now!*"

I walked out on wobbly legs and shut the door so softly it didn't completely close. I was heartsick. Nobody went to the principal's office unless they were being sent home. I didn't want to be delivered, along with the thank-you notes, back to Heart Colony.

I crept down the hallway, out the front door, and down all those cracked concrete steps.

There was a corner of the playground where nobody could see me from the main building. It was blocked by the elementary school's wall. Sitting on the splintered gray floor of the merry-go-round, I dragged my white canvas shoes along the sandy dirt circle until they were brownish red. Around and around, slow like a turtle I went, waiting for the elementary dismissal bell so I could be with Rachel, Adam, and Eli.

Can't go back to the colony and can't do what the outside world wants, either. Where was there left to go? *Can't feel God here, either.* I squinted my eyes up at the sun. Only the sun watched over the school building, and it didn't seem to do so very happily.

Finally I stopped moving the merry-go-round and stared glumly at the ground.

"Sarah Ruth?" Mrs. Monroe was standing over me.

"I hate school. I'm not going back in. You can't make me go."

"No one's going to make you go back in." Mrs. Monroe sat down beside me and sighed. "Besides, I don't much want to go back in, either. Too many rules. Too many snotty grown-ups who think they know everything when actually they know nothing at all."

I looked at her with surprise. Did she just say that? She was one of them. They were her people. Shouldn't she be agreeing with them?

"Mrs. Monroe?" I asked the question that always made me wonder. "Why didn't you get the sheriff to arrest Hezekiel when he fired at you with his gun?"

"Oh!" Mrs. Monroe giggled, then became quite serious. "Because Hezekiel had already served papers on me warning me not to 'trespass' on Heart Colony property." She shrugged. "So technically, I also was in the wrong.

"Individualism," Mrs. Monroe said then, and patted my arm. "I'll always remember you with that word."

"You, too," I said, smiling.

"I have to go back in." Mrs. Monroe sighed and glanced back at the big brick building. "But if you need me, I will help you. You just let me know. It's lovely out here, isn't it? A really nice day. I told them to let you sit out here, that you've been through a lot that they don't know about."

"Thanks." I smiled.

"Do you need me to call your mother?"

"No. I'll just wait out here until Adam, Eli, and Rachel come out. The school day is almost over, isn't it? My mother will be here soon."

"Maybe tomorrow will be better." Mrs. Monroe left me without agreeing, but I felt better all the same. Moments later it occurred to me that I had not even noticed what she was wearing today. A good while later it occurred to me that Mrs. Monroe was really more like us than she was like the others in that public school. She just didn't know it.

"Look!" Rachel was the first to come out. "The nurse gave me this for if I get sick." She held up a small white plastic thing with a nozzle and put it up to her mouth. "It helps me breathe better. It's an inhaler. It works better than standing in the food cellar!"

"What you doin' out here?" Adam dragged his book bag along the sand.

"Don't do that. Aunt Lila paid a lot of money for our school stuff," I said crossly.

"Look at your shoes," he answered, but he picked up the bag.

"Hurry, Eli." I waved impatiently. "I want to get out of here."

What a bad day. I wondered if the principal or any of the teachers had looked for me after I walked out. What if they told Aunt Lila I had been bad at school?

I was startled from my anguish by Adam's chortle of joy.

"It's Father!" He pointed down the end of the sidewalk to the figure of a man.

I saw the back of his head, the brown hair in the bowl style, the denim overalls, and what looked like Father's shoulders, but I couldn't be sure because the man suddenly was gone.

"Wait—Mother said to wait for her here."

Adam's feet left a smoky trail of playground dust, and Rachel and Eli joined the chase. All three of them disappeared around the corner of the elementary school building. I could do nothing but chase after them.

I ran past the corner and tripped over Adam's book bag. I saw Rachel's plastic breather lying broken on the ground. A big hand reached out and grabbed me. My heart thudded loudly in terror, then stopped. I heard a swishing sound in my ears, and for a moment, the world was spotted with black and gray.

Deacon Motes dragged me to the mud-dauber wagon, where Hezekiel was in the front seat guarding over my brothers and sister in the backseat. Deacon Caroll sat obediently behind the steering wheel, having done his job of pretending to be Father.

I thought about screaming, but I couldn't do that and struggle to keep out of the car. The terrified faces of my brothers and little sister convinced me I had to give in and go with them. It was my duty to comfort and later lead them in escape.

Deacon Motes and Hezekiel leaned over from the front seat and held us down by our necks until several miles past the town limits. We could sit up finally, Hezekiel said, if we behaved. The men's clothing still smelled of gasoline from the night before, but they had forgotten to put any in the car. They pulled into the orange Stop-and-Smile on the highway. We were not to move or make a sound.

Rachel was panting in short little gasps. She kept her head down, afraid to look at anyone. My brothers stared silently at me, as if they didn't know who I was. No means of escape or other clever ideas came to me.

All I could think about was how familiar the front of this store looked, and I didn't understand why.

Then a young attendant in an orange uniform and bright orange baseball cap approached the car. I knew that walk, those eyes, that shoulder that sloped lower than the other. *Think,* I pleaded to myself silently. *Think of a way to get his attention.* He leaned across to clean the windshield while the car filled with gas. I hoped they wouldn't notice the deep scar cutting across his forehead. He looked into the car and noticed me sitting behind Hezekiel and Deacon Motes.

He looked away and continued wiping off the windshield. He didn't jerk open the car door and come after Hezekiel with swinging fists. *Don't you love me, Joshua? Save me. Please help me.* My heart trembled.

He never looked at me again. He took the gas money from Deacon Caroll and walked off whistling!

All shaken up inside, I feared I'd never see my mother or the outside world again.

"We have to use the bathroom," I pleaded. I grabbed Rachel's hand and then lunged for the car door, jerking it partly open.

Hezekiel's claw hand dug into my shoulder, pulling me back. "Wait." He slammed the door shut. My shoulder ached with pain. As I looked out the car window, I saw Joshua washing off the windshield of an old blue tow truck. He was still whistling. My heart was breaking.

As we drove off, I noticed for the first time that Hezekiel's gun was lying across the chains in the back of the station wagon. My eyes grew wide with fear. *No wonder Joshua did not challenge them,* I thought. Or did he even care? What if he thought we were willingly going back to the colony?

As if we weren't even in the car, Hezekiel began talking about us to the other men.

"I gave instruction that you were only to watch the children today, not grab them. Tomorrow is our church meeting. Everything was planned for tomorrow, we were going to bring them in tomorrow. Now we'll have to work fast, because the papers haven't been served on their mother yet."

The rest of the ride to the colony was eerily silent.

16

THEY TOOK US to the schoolhouse. Adam and Eli looked a little worried. "They're going to make us go back to our old school?" Eli whispered unhappily.

Hezekiel and the men got out of the station wagon, but not before grabbing his gun and the chains from the rear compartment. In a matter of seconds, the chains were wrapped all around the vehicle and through the door handles, and we became prisoners inside Hezekiel's mud dauber while he and the men unlocked the chains from the schoolhouse and went inside for "important documents." They took the ignition keys with them.

Even though the windows were rolled down enough for us to breathe, it was suffocating in the car. Without the car keys, we couldn't operate the automatic windows to climb out, and the chains blocked the back door of the station wagon. I expected my younger brothers and sister to cry, but they didn't.

Silently we watched as Hezekiel and the two men came out of the school building with a big box. They unlocked the chains and car door momentarily to set the box in the front seat. Then they locked us back in and walked across the fields. I couldn't believe it. Hezekiel was not only headed to Widow Jacobs's house, he was taking his deacons with him!

I raised up for a moment and peered over the front seat. I saw my tape recorder in the box. The papers crammed in beside it looked like Mrs. Monroe's work sheets for history class.

Rachel exclaimed, "Look! A truck!"

When I turned my head to look, my heart skipped a joyful beat. There was the old blue tow truck coming slowly around the bend in the road by the latticework barn. It kept going, missing the turn to the schoolhouse, then stopped, backed up, and came driving straight toward us. My love, my most secret love, was coming to rescue me!

"It's that boy from the Pizza House," Rachel said. "The one you're in love with, Sarah Ruth."

"That's Joshua," Eli said. "Didn't you see the scar? He works at that gas station. Is he still your boyfriend, Sarah Ruth?"

Adam said nothing. He just looked at me and giggled while I fumed and turned very red.

Joshua drove the tow truck right up beside our car, then he looked down and saw the chains. He drove around in front of us, then backed up, the motor puttering loudly.

He was a wonderful driver. He had the back of that tow truck in perfect alignment with the front of our prison car.

We leaned forward anxiously, sweating with him as he began to hook up the tow. We watched intently, so intently that we did not see Deacon Caroll and Deacon Motes sneaking across from the schoolhouse field and up to the tow truck. The tow was fastened. Joshua waved to us and walked toward the cab of the truck, his back to us. Too late I saw the two men rise up from behind our station wagon. I threw myself across the front seat and pressed the horn, but Deacon Motes and Deacon Caroll were already leaping. Joshua was tackled from behind and taken down as we sat in the car gasping and afraid. His bright orange baseball cap went flying through the air and landed in the dirt. He put up a good fight, but Hezekiel came up with the gun.

Quickly Deacon Caroll unfastened the black belts and metal hook from the colony station wagon. In a matter of minutes, Deacon Motes was in the tow truck and Joshua was squished in the backseat with us. Not that I minded.

I felt really bad for him, not just for losing the fight but because as we watched it drive off, the wheels of the tow truck rolled right over his once clean "outsider" cap. He looked really sad.

When they took us to the church, I heard the fire

bell ringing in the distance, proclaiming our capture. I wrapped my arms around Rachel and Adam. "Mother will find us," I assured them. Eli tried to be brave but kept moving in closer to me and Joshua.

Caught off guard by the bell and still in their work clothes, the people of the congregation gathered in the church slowly. The Schumperts, Granny Abraham feebly hanging on Naomi's arm, my boy cousins, Mrs. Goode, Mary Helen—all of the colony—filling up the benches and pointing disapprovingly at our outsider appearance as we stood there in the front center aisle.

Father came in, his face pinching up in pain.

"What are they doing here?"

"It is what you ordered," Deacon Motes reminded him. He had the shotgun and kept it aimed at Joshua.

Horrified, I looked away. My father had done this to us? I wanted to shake my head in disbelief. Like my mother at the gas spill, I pretended something else had been said, something of my own choosing, something nicer to my heart.

"Why are you using a gun? And inside a church?" I could hear my father but couldn't bring myself to look at him. I know he was now standing in the third row and close to the center aisle.

"We had to use the gun to stop this one from taking your children back to the outside world," Deacon Caroll said, almost ashamedly, as if he realized suddenly this was all wrong. "You remember Joshua and what he did, don't you?"

Hezekiel came down the aisle with the box labeled COURT DOCUMENTS and the big board he used for beating my boy cousins. "Brother Heart, the last time you were in church, didn't you say you wished to bring your children home?"

"Yes." But Father was clearly unhappy.

"You asked us to help you bring them home."

"The children belong with their mother."

"That isn't what you said. You said, 'Go bring them to me.' I wouldn't have done it if I had known you weren't sure about it."

Deacon Motes looked uncomfortable. "We don't snatch children up. You ordered this done, and you are their father. You have custody of them under our church laws, which are the same in outside courts as well."

"I didn't think you would do this. I didn't say go do it now. I didn't say use a gun. I didn't say do it against their will."

"But you did tell us to."

"Yes." Father shook his head sadly. "I love them and I missed them."

When he looked over at me, I saw regretful tears. I realized he did still love us.

"But I made a mistake telling you that. I want you to take them back to their mother." Father's voice deepened almost to a growl. "I took the beatings for them the first time they left. I will take them again now. Don't hit my children. Let them go and then I, too, will go, to be with them and their mother."

Hezekiel nodded to Deacon Motes, and suddenly the shotgun was aimed at Father.

"Then you are not a member of this church, and you

do not want your children brought up in this church."

"Then I am not a member."

"If you are not a member, then you are trespassing." Hezekiel's evil face shone with cunning. "We can have you arrested and jailed."

My brothers and sister uttered frightened noises, and Rachel started to cry.

"Don't you want him to go to jail?" Hezekiel turned to them.

They shook their heads no.

"If you don't want him to go to jail," Hezekiel wheedled, "then you have to rejoin our church. You have to stand right over here and say you want to be in Heart Colony church. It is, after all, your church. It has your name."

"Don't do it." I squeezed their hands. Something about the way Hezekiel was guiding them to do this—something was out of place, wrong. I tried thinking ahead of him but couldn't.

"This isn't what I want." Father's voice was anguished.

"Yes, it is," Hezekiel said angrily. "Only, you are too much of a coward to finish what you started, and now we have to finish it for you." He turned toward us again. "What do you want to do, children?"

"I want to be in Heart Colony church," Rachel said in a whispery voice.

"Over here, where God can see you." Hezekiel impatiently moved her toward the first bench. The gun was aimed away from Father, but he wasn't allowed to move. Deacon Caroll stood guard nearby. Adam and Eli faced the crowd and proclaimed, just as timidly, "I want to be in Heart Colony church."

"Louder!" Hezekiel made all three of them repeat it.

"Now you."

I shook my head no. Deacon Motes raised the gun to Father's head again. Rachel, Adam, and Eli begged me tearfully with their eyes. Reluctantly I moved forward to the first bench. All the people were staring at me. It was worse than the spelling bee. I couldn't look at their faces and say what I hated hearing from my mouth.

Then I saw it. My tape recorder had been placed under the bench. The REWIND button was down and the tape was spinning silently.

"You have a tape recorder under the bench." I stepped back and pointed.

Hezekiel swooped down and picked it up. He jammed a button to make it stop, then held it up to the congregation. "I have the Devil's creation doing God's work."

The people in the church nodded affirmatively but were clearly puzzled.

Hezekiel turned to Father. "Everything you admitted about ordering us to take your children is on here."

The famous claw came up into the air. He turned to us. *Stomp* went his left foot, and then *stomp* went the right. He no longer scared me. The badly acted stance was ridiculous. "Your desire to be raised in our church is on here. Lawyers from SlapEasy won't be able to give you back to your mother *or* your father, unless your father stays here."

My brothers and sister started crying again. Even Eli was wailing loudly. Joshua was clenching his fists tight.

"You don't have us on that tape," I said bravely.

"You see the tape recorder."

"I see no buttons pushed down. To get our voices you would have to push the fourth button down." Now I would find out just how much they knew about that tape recorder.

"We had the fourth button pushed down," Mary Helen said with a sneer. "I'm the one who showed him. The fourth button says *voices.*"

Thank goodness Hezekiel had always kept Mary Helen out of school.

"I don't think you pushed it down, and if you don't have our voices on there, *you* will be going to jail."

The people in the back started talking softly, then a worried murmur traveled along the benches to the front, stopping where the guilty driver and helpers sat. They looked up questioningly at Hezekiel.

"Quiet!" Hezekiel shouted.

The main door to the church opened, and Joshua's parents walked in. "Why did you ring the church bells?" his father asked.

"These children have come back to our church."

Mrs. Mueller saw her son and gasped. Joshua turned his head so as not to look at her.

"We were kidnapped," I said, "and everybody that

takes part in this will be going to jail. My mother will be calling the sheriff."

"They weren't kidnapped," Hezekiel shouted over the loudly doubting congregation. "We have proof. The sheriff has no jurisdiction over me or us."

"Let's hear that thing." Deacon Motes was nervous and pointed the shotgun at the tape recorder. The other men up front nodded in agreement.

"Mary Helen," Hezekiel called to her. He set the tape recorder down and picked up the beating board. "After we've heard the voices, I have punishment for those who wish to be forgiven." He looked straight into my eyes.

Mary Helen swayed to the front, her fat roll punched out around the waist of her skirt. She thought she was Miss *Smart* Colony, and I couldn't wait.

She pushed a button. Everyone leaned forward. Nothing happened.

She glanced back at her father, and I knew it was my only chance. I grabbed the recorder and ran.

Mary Helen's properly sewn sleeve restricted her arm from moving fast enough. The tape recorder was all mine, and I traveled hurriedly back down the aisle, telling everyone that soon they would hear the truth from Hezekiel's own captured words to Beth Jacobs. Hezekiel tried to chase after me with the beating board, but my father knocked him down. I turned and saw Deacon Motes aim the shotgun at Father again.

"Devil box! Stop it!" Hezekiel screeched, the claw in midair.

I pushed the PLAY button.

"It must be rats or mice." I heard my voice from so long ago.

Anxiously I watched the black ribbon moving slowly. *Oh, when will it get to Hezekiel's voice?*

Just then my nasty cousin knocked the tape recorder from my hands. We wrestled over it on the floor of the church, until, once again, Joshua came to my rescue.

So now there were three of us rolling on the church floor fighting over a tape recorder, and one of us was really fat. I couldn't throw Mary Helen off me, and then it was just two of them fighting over the tape recorder while the noise in the congregation grew to a roar of disapproval at us. I don't know what he did to her, but Mary Helen screamed like the day he gave her the frog, and suddenly my Joshua held up the tape recorder.

The left side door of the church opened, and Mother and Aunt Lila were standing there with Mrs. Monroe. I could see Mrs. Monroe's car parked beside the tow truck. Joshua ran out of the church, his hands clutching the Devil box, and everybody piled out after.

There was shouting and screaming and everybody running everywhere, but Joshua had the lead. Suddenly a shot rang out, and I saw him fall.

As if we were all playing stone tag, everybody stood still.

"Stop or I'll shoot again." Hezekiel's voice rang out

from the top of the single stairs. He aimed the shotgun high. Father looked up helplessly. I glanced back at Joshua. He was standing up. A small trickle of blood was soaking down the sleeve of his shirt from where the fired shot had barely clipped him. Joshua's mother started sobbing, and Mary Helen sauntered over to my hero. For a moment I felt again that jealous rage that I'd felt that day she fell over the jar of paint. How dare she tend to the wounds of my boyfriend? But as she neared him, it became clear she had no plans of goodwill toward Joshua at all. She had something to do, and she intended on doing it. She didn't take the tape recorder. She took the tape. Then, standing away from us, she pulled out the long tape ribbon and held it taut between her hands, to break it apart in several places.

"What are you doing?" Hezekiel screamed at her. "Now how can we get their confessions for court? You are stupid, like your mother."

That's all it took for Aunt Lila. We heard that slap coming from a mile away, and I don't know how she angled it past that gun. But she got him, and it would have been a real throw-down right there between husband and wife if it hadn't been for Deacon Motes and Deacon Caroll pulling her away.

Hezekiel waved the shotgun all around him. But everybody kept staring at the red imprint of Aunt Lila's hand on his face.

"Now, Deacon Schumpert will prepare some affadavits for everyone to sign. You see these people have trespassed on our property. That one"—he pointed to

Aunt Lila—"committed aggravated assault *and* battery. Deacon Randolph, go to my house and call the sheriff. We will hold the trespassers until the law can get out here."

Deacon Randolph did not move. Mother put her arm around Rachel, and Father put his arm around Mother. Although I was shaking in my canvas shoes, I had to smile.

"Go call!" Hezekiel ordered. Deacon Randolph hesitated, then ran.

"There's no need for a gun," my father said. "A gun is used only to protect the colony from outsiders, not to turn us into outsiders who shoot and kill one another." Many of the deacons murmured in agreement with my father's words.

Joshua stared up at Hezekiel's gun and walked slowly toward him up the steps until the gun was nearly level with his head and just inches away. He was shaking visibly, whether from fear or rage, I'll never know.

Just like I'll never know why I did such a foolish thing as to go stand beside Joshua. But I did.

My mother and father came up beside me, and then Joshua's parents took the bottom stairs. Joshua's mother ripped a strip off her sleeve and reached up to bandage where the shotgun shell had grazed Joshua's arm. He shrugged her hand off. She began crying, until his blood-streaked hand reached back to clasp hers. He never took his eyes off Hezekiel.

I could feel movement behind me, but didn't know

how many had moved to face Hezekiel's gun. I only knew that the steps were getting mighty crowded. The group standing under the tree was growing smaller.

"I didn't set fire to the Schumpert house, and you know it," Joshua finally spoke.

"That was your planned sign from God, the fire," I said quickly, for Hezekiel's finger had moved toward the gun's trigger. My heart was exploding high in my chest. "That's what was on that tape."

"You sent me to the Schumperts' shed for a shovel, then locked me in."

Behind Joshua the congregation gasped.

"You started the fire and made sure the hose and the buckets were off the water truck, so Father would be blamed as well." I clutched Joshua's free hand for support. It felt delicious in mine.

"Don't listen to the Devil's child!" Hezekiel shouted.

"The buckets were at our house that day. Our father took them off the water truck," my cousin Daniel suddenly spoke from under the tree. "If we told anyone, we would have been beaten. He hid the fire hose. It's true."

The congregation gasped again.

"I did not lock Joshua in the shed." Hezekiel spread his hands out and looked over the congregation, the shotgun still in his clutch. "I told him to go in the shed and get the shovel, then I saw the fire in the house and I yelled at him to fetch the others. I thought he was gone, and I threw the matches and kerosene I'd been carrying into the shed and locked it. I had those matches and kerosene to burn out some poison oak over yonder by the Schumperts' house. Now, you know you asked me to burn out those weeds in that ditch." He appealed to the Schumperts.

They came over to the steps. Mr. Schumpert showed no emotion, but Naomi was furious. "You almost killed Granny Abraham," she screamed at Hezekiel.

"If I had known she was in there, I would not have watched the fire grow so big before going in. I was scared to go in, but I did it to save her. Your house burned because of bad wires. I told your husband once before that he overloads the wires, and he did not let me fix it. You had a fire like that once before." Hezekiel pointed angrily at her, causing her to agree, even in her fury.

Deacon Motes let go of Aunt Lila's arm and moved over to the stairs. "You are not a man of God if you burned that house. You disgust all of us who followed and believed in you."

"I did not start that fire," Hezekiel insisted. "All I did was not stop it when I saw what was to be. God started that fire, so you could be warned. I was chosen to be your leader."

"We lost nearly everything," Naomi said sadly, leaning against her husband. "The quilts, my father's tools, our family lists."

"You're lucky I came by." Hezekiel couldn't help but notice the angry glares cast in his direction. I could feel them from where I was standing. "I was going to burn the lattice barn, that one colony vanity that truly upsets God by its presence. I had everything with me, but then I saw the true fire and I set my fire stuff in their shed. If I had not happened by for a shovel, Granny Abraham would have died."

"I don't believe you." Mr. Schumpert's face was tense, gray, as though sick. "My wiring could have started the fire, I allow it. It has happened before. But you helped it along. You put kerosene on that fire, and you did it because you knew I had found bank papers of your secret account in SlapEasy."

The congregation groaned loudly. The last of the supporters moved out from under the tree and over to the left side of the steps with us. All but Hezekiel's sons and Mary Helen.

"Show me those papers," Hezekiel said slyly.

I reached down and jerked out part of the front hem of my dress. The picture of Joshua fell out and landed on his foot. I could have died. Quickly I scooped it up, and the folded white papers. But I only held out the folded white papers. *"Deposit only. Hezekiel Whittenstone. SlapEasy Bank of Progress,"* I read.

My father put his hand on my shoulder protectively, and I passed the papers to him for all to see.

"You had the money, but you were going to blame me." Aunt Lila squeezed her way up to the top of the steps beside me to face Hezekiel again.

Beth Jacobs walked up to the church lawn and regarded the crowd with standoffish bemusement. Hezekiel seemed to get renewed strength from her presence.

"That tractor money was *owed* to me," Hezekiel shouted. "My father was killed because the colony sent him to SlapEasy for tractor parts. My father became a martyr for the colony because I was destined to become the leader. The tractor money was blood money."

"It *is* blood money," Father said angrily. "The blood of James Ackerman, who should have been on a new tractor."

"He died instantly." Joshua spoke up. "It made no difference that the car was in SlapEasy when it happened. Hezekiel made the ambulance take Mr. Ackerman, even though he was dead and there was no hope."

Mrs. Randolph put her arm around her newly adopted son as they stood near the steps. "Eric will have to be baptized by the hand of God, not the hand of Satan's messenger. Hezekiel must no longer be a leader of our church, nor a member of Heart Colony."

Samuel Lawrence helped old Mrs. Goode up the crowded steps. She pushed past me, nearly knocking me back down another step with her bony little body. Mrs. Goode smiled at Hezekiel as though he were only a bad little boy.

"We do not have a vindictive God. Our God is a just and mighty God, full of forgiveness," she chided. "In the Gospel of Jesus, He offers redemption. So must we. Hezekiel will stay, but not as leader. He must take his punishments and then be forgiven. It's in our Bible, although he stapled that section shut."

Alarmed, I realized Hezekiel must have found my

stapler, Mrs. Monroe's stapler, to do the Bible work.

People shook their heads at Mrs. Goode in disagreement.

"It is our way," Samuel Lawrence reminded everyone gently, but not too gladly.

"It is my *duty* to be leader. God chose me. I have done nothing wrong." Hezekiel faced us defiantly. "I will start a new colony. Those that wish to follow and be God's favorites, come with me now."

Mary Helen was the first to push through us and run toward him, but he shoved her away. "It's your fault. You didn't get their voices on the tape recorder, and you ruined the tape so it couldn't be used. Look what you've done to me. You are just like—" Then, eyeing Aunt Lila so nearby, he stopped.

Mary Helen grabbed at her father's hand, but he jerked it away. I would have felt sorry for her, except I didn't believe in lying, especially to myself.

"I can't build a new colony without my boys." He motioned to them under the tree.

The littlest one, Isaiah, shook violently, but all eight remained standing where they were. At last Daniel walked over to the steps. He faced his father without flinching. "We're not going. We want to live with Mother."

With a cry of anguish, Hezekiel snatched up the shotgun and aimed it at his son's heart. "You're going with me."

"That's enough of this," Deacon Randolph shouted. He was trembling with anger. "Put that gun away."

"I'd rather he shoot me," Daniel said. "If I go with him, all he'll do is beat me until I'm dead, anyway."

I was reminded of the favorite Bible story my father liked to tell, only this Daniel was facing the truth, not a hungry lion. Still, he remained strong hearted, and surely God was with him, for Hezekiel started crying, then slowly lowered the gun. His finger finally released from the trigger. "It was because I loved you," he said. "Someday you'll understand."

No longer proud and powerful, he was nonetheless unrepentant. "I grew up with no father because of this colony, and now you have seen that I will have no children." He turned and motioned impatiently to his one colony vanity. "She is going with me. I brought her here. She belongs to me."

There was a shocked murmur of whispers as Beth Jacobs moved gracefully up the steps to him. "You are no longer a leader, and you do not own me."

Aunt Lila regarded her with contempt. "Now that he is not leader, you do not want my husband."

Beth Jacobs faced all of us with a graceful fury. "I came here to be a teacher, but your petty jealousy left me with no friends and no job. It was as if I were imprisoned. I am going home to my own colony, a colony where I can have *fun*."

She wanted nothing more to do with any of us, it was obvious from the way she exited the church, and the imagined definition of "fun" raised a few eyebrows, especially Mother's and Aunt Lila's.

"Solomon Heart, I regret what has transpired here,"

Deacon Motes said, moving to stand next to my father. "I am sorry I followed under Hezekiel's direction and caused grief to you and your children." He patted Rachel on the head, but she remained wide-eyed with fright.

"I, too, am sorry," Deacon Randolph said, walking up to the crowd.

"Did you make that phone call for me?" Hezekiel asked anxiously.

"Yes," Deacon Randolph said. "I called the sheriff especially for you. I will sign papers on your liberal use of a weapon within the churchyard. The sheriff should be here very soon now. If you wish to leave before then, I will not stop you. But I never wish to see you in Heart Colony again."

"I am truly remorseful over James Ackerman's death," Hezekiel said as he ducked back into the church. Everyone began filing back through the left-side church doors toward him. Then it started, the slow stomping of the feet. I wasn't stomping. I was just following everybody else, curious as to where Hezekiel would go. I wondered if he'd make one last stand to control everything that was now out of control, especially since he was in his controlling building. But he didn't. He took the coward's way out. The stomping of feet grew louder and moved quickly toward him.

The last I saw of my uncle Hezekiel Whittenstone, ex-leader of Heart Colony, he was running like a rabbit through the door and down the steps of the right side of the church while people were still filing in through the left.

He left us with one ominous warning. "Try to get through the winter without any money," he cried. "You'll wish you had kept me as leader."

A CURIOUS SUNSET decorated the hills of Heart Colony, red and blue from the lights of the screaming sheriff cars, yellow from the bouquet Joshua quickly picked for me, and peach from Mother's dress, which Father suddenly noticed had been stripped of the shiny buttons and taken down to a proper Mennonite length as a compromise—but was modern all the same.

Aunt Lila's vacation from nine children was over, and Mary Helen's introduction to manners was just beginning. In fact, right after Hezekiel left, Aunt Lila marched over to the nearest bush and took a keen switch to Mary Helen's backside, right there in the churchyard in front of everybody. It was the first time I could recall Mary Helen ever getting whipped.

Aunt Lila returned to SlapEasy with all her children and several years later married the fireman named Tim. We remained in the colony and watched it become a place of happy worship and simple blessings once again. Gone were all the punishments.

Because Father turned it down, Mr. Schumpert became the new leader and inherited Hezekiel's house. He and Father cut the chains off the school, and we cleaned it up so nicely for Mrs. Monroe that she barely recognized it. The next year we had to add on a room, and I became the assistant teacher. I brought back Mrs. Monroe's gleaming silver stapler, and she told me to keep it on my teacher's desk.

The first letter to arrive in our new colony mailboxes was to Mother from Cousin Amelia. Inside the envelope the letter had been sewn into a pocket lining, and even Father had to laugh. The second letter was from Cassie, asking when she could visit. She and her mother came out the following Sunday. I could count on Cassie to buy two cakes whenever we took food into SlapEasy for bake sales. She said we were the best cooks in the whole South, even better than the ones at the school cafeteria. I don't know if it's true about the South, but I know it's true about the cafeteria, and I also know that whenever we set up our canopy in town, everything sells out quickly. It was because of our bake sales that we were able to buy a used fire truck with a nice long hose permanently attached.

The one-hundred-dollar savings-bond prize from the spelling bee was framed by my father and honors the front hall of our house. I never knew what happened to my uncle Hezekiel or to Beth Jacobs. I'm sure they went their separate ways. I'm also sure that Mother and Aunt Lila did something to Hezekiel's illicit bank account the day of our kidnapping, because despite what Hezekiel predicted, Heart Colony had plenty of money for the winter, *and* a new tractor. James Ackerman's name is inscribed on it.

I am eighteen now and will graduate soon from Mrs. Monroe's busy two-room school. Mrs. Monroe wants me to go to a Mennonite college, but right now I have no plans. Although I rejoined the church, leaving Heart Colony sometimes crosses my mind. The colony is once again like all other honorable Mennonite colonies, true to my deepest faith and beliefs, and with plenty of room for individualism. But there's one temptation in SlapEasy that appeals to me, and he says he'll be waiting. Joshua. J-o-s-h-u-a. My most favorite spelling word of all.